Power Lines
and Other Stories

Power Lines
and Other Stories

Jane Bradley

The University of Arkansas Press

Fayetteville / London // 1989

Designer: Chiquita Babb
Typeface: Linotron 202 Garamond #3
Typesetter: G & S Typesetters, Inc.
Printer: Braun-Brumfield, Inc.
Binder: Braun-Brumfield, Inc.

The paper used in this publication meets the minimum
requirements of the American National Standard for
Permanence of Paper for Printed Library Materials
Z39.48-1984. ∞

Stories in this collection have appeared, in slightly different form, in the following journals: "Power Lines" (*The Literary Review,* forthcoming), "Across the Road" (*Kansas Quarterly,* Summer,
1987), "Twirling" (*The North American Review,* Winter, 1986), "What
Happened to Wendell?" (*Crazyhorse,* Vol. 24, Spring, 1983), "Mistletoe" (*The Virginia Quarterly Review,* Winter, 1986, reprinted by
the University of South Carolina Press, *New Writing by Southern
Women*), "Noises" (*Sou'wester,* Spring, 1986), "Blue Sky" (*Confronta-
tion,* Spring & Fall, 1987), and "The Evil Side of Red Brown" (*Colum-
bia,* Vol. 7, 1982).

Library of Congress Cataloging-in-Publication Data

Bradley, Jane, 1955 –
     Power lines and other stories / Jane Bradley.
         p.   cm.
     ISBN 1-55728-110-6 (alk. paper)
     ISBN 1-55728-111-4 (pbk. : alk. paper)
     1. Women—Fiction.   I. Title.
PS3552.R2274P6   1989
813'.54—dc19   89-31238
                                                   CIP

Contents

Power Lines
and Other Stories

Mistletoe

I know I am not dead because I see her running toward me now. Her red hair fans out in this cold gray morning air, her green coat flaps open letting the breeze wrap around her chest, and her shoe laces fly untied slapping her ankles as she runs across this scrubby, frost-covered yard.

I stand by the truck here waiting with my baby, Darly, wrapped around my hip, and Mitch sits over there with the engine revving up, dying down, and revving again, he says to keep the engine turning, but I know it's to churn the quiet morning air into nothing but noise. To ease his pushing, I ran from the house with Darly bouncing, laughing on my hip, and I yelled to Marta, "Hurry, Daddy's waiting," and she comes fast now because even at six years old she knows not to make a man like him wait.

She runs, and I watch the white vapor float from her mouth, and I see she is like me with my red hair, my dark green eyes, and my way of running with my mouth wide open, my arms flying, but my legs steady and fast. I'm afraid I've shaped her so like myself that she, too, will live a life underwater while others breathe the sharp real air.

I can see it has started. Already she loves old story books and pictures of the long dead who stare in a black and white trance. Already she collects dried weeds and rocks worn to odd shapes and colors rarely seen above ground. And she does odd things like the way each morning she picks a fairy tale to live by. She plays out the parts and pretends the world is just a story that's been written and has to be lived through to the end. Already her teachers call her deep. I never wanted a deep child. I just wanted a happy one who ran and laughed like all the other giggling girls.

As she slips past me and climbs up into the truck now, I see the aluminum foil package hiding in her pocket, and I know she is Gretel today, and she will get safely lost in the woods. I smell the thick sweetness of the powdered doughnuts she has tucked under her arm for the ride. Darly smells the sweetness too, and she kicks her legs and bounces as she watches Marta scoot across the seat and settle next to Mitch. "You want a doughnut, Darly?" Marta says, and before I can say no, Darly has the white cake crumbling in her fat hand. As she sucks the sugar, her feet kick and her eyes shine.

We are bouncing down the driveway now, and I am happy for a moment because I will finally have some of that mistletoe Dean once showed me, and I will hang it all through my little white house. I will see the lake again, the green-brown water where Dean taught me to hook a bass and clean it and eat it right there in the woods. He laughed to see me in big paint-splotched man's khaki pants, flannel shirt, and old brogans. Dean said he liked to see a woman in man's clothes because it made what was hid underneath a sweeter surprise.

"You know where you're going?" Mitch says, and I smell his cigarette, the doughnuts, and the oily old tools in his truck.

"Yes," I say. "You head up 58 Highway to Sparky's Bait Shop. Take a quick left. I'll know the dirt road when I see it."

"What makes you know so much about dirt roads?" he says, looking straight ahead and frowning out from under his cap.

"I grew up in this town too," I say. "I know all about dirt roads and mountains and streams."

"I bet you do," he says.

I tap Marta's shoulder. "There's a cave out near Sweetwater that's big enough to fly a plane around in."

"Let's go," she says.

"One day," I say, and I look out the window at the stark brown trees whizzing by, and I think this ride will not be long enough. With Mitch there driving like a machine, Marta gazing out at the highway dreaming, and Darly's little mind drawn into the way her pink wet fingers can vanish in the white doughnut and come out full of crumbs, having them all with me locked into their own worlds, inside this black truck, I would like to listen to the sound of this old engine and watch forever the woods as they stand there so thick and straight. I see a dark bird swoop down in the branches, a flash of shadow, then it's gone as the truck pulls us toward that cold gray lake where mistletoe grows now with green leaves and white berries full of poison sap.

Seven years is a long time to love a man who isn't yours. He had Mildred with her dyed blue-black hair, her hips wide as a Christmas table, and I had, still have, Mitch. And my girls. It's the girls who make this living something I can stand, and I know if Dean could have had a kid, he would have gone on living. I kept hoping he would have one with me with this body so rich I have to push Mitch away from me sometimes for fear he will plant another seed in me. I push because I know that sometimes life rushes through and takes hold in spite of all my efforts to make it stop. I still hurt for those two I wouldn't let come, but to let them come would have killed me for certain in a way nobody can see. So I went to the doctor who said things like "Terminate. Terminate the pregnancy." What words we find sometimes. But Marta was a wanted child. I wanted her when Mitch didn't because I had to invent something to keep me from flying off this earth like a mist vanishing in the sun. So I pushed for my Marta, and she holds me here still.

Darly was his all out effort to get a boy, a son to hand down a name. If you ask me, Mitchell Stone isn't worth saving. So when that baby pushed through my blood to be a girl, I laughed out loud and yelled, "That's my darlin'. That's my girl."

I wanted them to tie my tubes right then because I didn't want more chances, but they put me off saying it's a serious thing for a woman healthy and young as me.

"But I swear I don't want no more," I said.

And they said, "But what if? What if?" And they got me thinking a child is all. And what if? What if, and my body was all tied up and dry as a rock. So I waited and I pushed Mitch off and I tried pills and they made me see spots, and I tried copper wires and they made me bleed like a pig, and I tried all those rubber things and creams. And I've pushed him off as much as I could.

But with Dean I opened all skin, bone, and muscle, and when I loved him I was so happy I wasn't tied up inside because I wanted his seed to grow. Dean moved in me like a warm river, and you'd have thought we'd grow a thousand babies.

Suddenly I see we've just passed the bait shop, and he is about to miss the turn. "Right here," I yell, pointing, and he jerks the wheel, bouncing me and Marta and Darly. The doughnuts go flying, but we make the turn and bounce down this road toward the lake where Dean and I walked through the trees, where we slid his aluminum fishing boat in the water, cast our lures for a fat bright fish we could clean and cook on the spot with his little Sterno stove. He always brought the corn meal and the lard and the salt, all packed neatly in old peanut butter jars. He planned for everything, never forgot the napkins, forks, nothing. He always said, "It's got to be just right." And it was. It was until that little bit of blood pushed through the wrong place in his head and busted my life wide open.

Mitch looks out frowning. "Where is this place you claim mistletoe grows thick as trees?"

"On down a bit," I say.

"How do you know what's growing here?" He looks straight ahead the way he always looks when he asks me what might be a dangerous question.

"I hear things," I say, and I pat Marta's leg. "This is going to be so pretty."

He pulls a cigarette from his shirt pocket. "I don't know what's wrong with getting it where you always do. That ridge behind our house is full of the stuff waiting to be shot down."

"This place is pretty," I say. "The girls need a little trip, and there's not much else to do on a Sunday morning." He looks at his watch, and I know he's thinking he wants to be home in time to watch some football game. "Neighbors have shot down most of that mistletoe on the ridge," I say. "And we've got to have some in our house for Christmas."

"Yeah, I want kisses," Marta says laughing.

I pat her and say, "Shh," fearing her high happy voice will wake Darly who is now sleeping on my chest. I look at Mitch and say low and hard, "I don't want to have to buy it at the store."

He shakes his head. "Only thing crazier than shooting leaves off a tree is paying good money to buy a bunch of dead ones at the store."

"Who knows," I say, "Maybe you'll see something live you can kill."

He looks down at Marta and gives that grin he gives only to Marta. He loves her, and I know it. "You want rabbit stew for supper tonight?" he says.

Marta covers her mouth with her hand and stares up. "You won't kill a rabbit, Daddy," she says.

"Rabbit's good," he says. "Mmmm mmm."

"Momma, he won't," Marta says.

I say, "Hush, Darly's stirring." And he rubs Marta's red head, and she looks up at him and grins.

The truck slows, and I see the road has ended in a wide patch of black dirt worn hard by so many cars and trucks parking, and tents standing, and kids playing, and boats going in and out of the water. It was early summer the last time with Dean, with the trees all green and breezy and the water warm and wavy full of bugs riding the surface, fish swimming under, and birds flying all around. "I'll bring you back Christmas," he said.

Mitch stops the truck and pushes the door open and heads for the trees. His gun is still here, so I know it's not that he's eager to shoot mistletoe. Marta has slipped out of the truck like a mouse, and now she stands by that icy dark water and looks out. Any other girl would be running and squealing and throwing rocks, but Marta stands there like she knows something has happened here more than camping and fishing and barbecue. And it did. I lived here awhile, lived more than in all my years growing and playing, and working. Here I didn't live underwater. Here I heard and smelled and felt this world the way I should.

Mitch is back now, and he walks the edge of the water, looking out, waiting, knowing Marta likes her quiet and I'm not ready. He watches her from a distance as if she's a wild bird that will fly off if he moves. He shoves his hands in his pockets and squints against the cold wind off the water.

Sometimes I think he must know it was Dean who brought me here. It was Dean who would point out the high mistletoe with his sharp eyes. He could name a bird before I even saw it. He could spot a brown fish against a muddy lake bottom and name a tree by the smell of its leaves in the breeze. It was spring when he promised, "We'll come back in December and get mistletoe for you to hang all around and have kisses wherever you turn." But we never came back. He had his Mildred. He kept saying he'd leave her. He kept saying he loved me, but he had to stay a little longer. She had problems that held him hard: her momma died, her daddy died. She had operations, bad nerves, high sugar, low blood, something always, and he couldn't leave her alone. He kept waiting, and he promised, he promised, but she kept slipping back just when I thought he was ready to go. Then he had his stroke.

Stroke. A right word for it, like something rises up and slaps you down, and you don't even have the chance to ask, "How?" It just slams from the inside out. Stroke. He had it, then he couldn't move to fish or drive or hunt green leaves in tree tops. No. He could move just enough to get across his room. He could hardly talk with his mouth half frozen and his brain slowed, and his left arm and leg so weak, just moving on his bed would make him sweat. But he fought hard for living just long enough so he could finally move to hold the gun with one hand and blast his pain to nothing at all.

Dean had green eyes too, and green eyes always made me look long because they're kind of rare when you think of all the brown and blue eyes staring out at this world. Green eyes always make me stop and think, "Yes, I know how green eyes see." That's why when I watch Marta looking out, I can feel some living air move. She could have been Dean's with those eyes, but they are my green eyes no doubt. Dean didn't leave a mark in this world except for what he left pressed deep in my body, my heart, my tangled mind.

Darly stirs against my chest and suddenly opens her eyes wide as she looks at me. "Momma!" she says as if I've been gone for days.

"Let's see the trees," I say, and I step out of the truck and feel the leaves crunch under my feet, and I sigh out loud with the cold opening my head to the smells of dirt and water.

Mitch looks at me with a look so flat he might as well be looking at the trees, and he turns back to squinting at the gray water. Marta is so busy poking sticks in the mud she has no thought of what I might be doing now. A child, she just slides through living like it's a long truck ride. Darly whines, and I pull her bottle from my pocket and stick it in her mouth, and she sighs and sucks and closes her eyes.

I give her a squeeze and head toward that path along the sycamores to where a stand of oaks grow so shady and full that squirrels run year round and people can lay back cool and hidden from the summer sun. But it's cold in these woods now, and the ground hard as rock. Darly snuggles closer and peers out, but I don't mind the cold because if it were warm and green here now, I couldn't stand it. Five months isn't long enough to stop grieving, not five years, not five hundred years. So I'm cold and my arms ache from the weight of Darly, but the pain feels right to me. Now I see the spot where we cooked our fish and ate our bread and lay back on his old sleeping bag, and stared up at the trees. I look up through those scraggly black branches that reach like dark veins across the sky, and I try to remember the way the smell of dirt fills your head when you're lying with your back on the ground. Looking close, I see that mistletoe creeping along the branches, drawing its own life from these giant trees.

I hear them rushing up behind me now, Marta with her feet stirring up as much noise as a child can make, and Mitch with those long smooth man's steps you can hardly hear. They are a hunter's steps, light but firm and sure. I look around and see his shotgun swinging low to the ground.

"Here," he says, gruff and flat as a cough.

"This is the place," I say, staring up to where those leaves grow bunchy and green in the high sunlight. I say, "This is the place," but he can't know what I'm saying when he looks up and sees simple green leaves waving there in the breeze. All he has to do is pull that trigger and the buckshot will splatter into the trees, and he will be happy with himself for shutting me up about what I want, and he will drive us straight home. Mitch sees a thing up there, a thing he can have by simply knocking it down.

Even Marta sees this place is more than what she sees with her eyes. She has scattered the cornbread she hid in her pocket, and she has made a little trail of bread crumbs along the path while playing her game.

Even Darly sees more to this place than Mitch who walks around now squinting up seeing only where to shoot. Darly squirms against me, laughs, and points at things nobody can see. Babies do that, they live in a double world, and they talk and laugh and cry at things we'll never know. Old people do it too. And of course the crazy ones who wander the streets. I'd rather be a wild-eyed crazy woman who talks to fast voices and sees panthers in shadows or stars on her ceiling, sees fiery closets or jerky hands moving with a will of their own. I'd rather see madness than to see the world through the flat eyes of a man like Mitch who just lives to sleep and eat.

Marta is talking to me now, but I can't hear her for my thinking. I see she's walking in her private little paths through the trees and scattering crumbs as she speaks. I hate to miss a word she says because I know words are sometimes all we have to claim a little life, so when I miss something said, I want to cry. Sometimes I wish I could be all eyes, ears, hands holding all to see, but then I know it's easier and it don't hurt so if I can just shut down and stare at the world like it's an old bad movie I've seen a hundred times.

We're all watching him now, walking in wide circles under these trees as he looks up, takes aim, walks a little more, takes aim again.

"Don't you shoot any birds, Daddy," Marta says.

Darly bounces and points. "Bird," she says in her thick baby voice that flattens any meaning to sweet simple sound.

Mitch aims, then grins at Marta. "Don't you want bird soup? Witches eat bird soup," he says. She laughs with him but stares up at those trees with a warning on her face.

"He won't hurt nothing," I say, and he frowns at me.

Dean knew the meaning of mistletoe like most men don't. When we talked of hanging it all through my house, he'd laugh and say, "One man's kiss is another man's poison," because he knew Mitch was sure to dodge those green branches like they were hives full of bees.

He takes aim again now, and his quick nod tells me he's ready, so with one hand I pull Marta back. "Cover your ears," I say, and I kneel on the ground with Darly squeezed against my thighs and I cover her ears and hold her face to my chest and pull her in as best as I can to keep her from hearing the blast that will shake these woods deeper than any storm. Marta stands there in front of me with her red chapped hands pressing her red hair against her ears. Her jeans are muddy at the cuffs and droop around her sneakers black from the lake's dirt, sad-looking and wet with shoelaces still untied and dragging in the leaves. But her red hair catches the light from the sun even down here in the dark woods, and I see bright threads of gold sparkle as she tosses her head back to see up through the trees.

Mitch gives us a look to make sure we are ready, and he raises his gun. He squints up and his fingers reach.

"Fly birds!" Marta yells. "Fly away! Fly away!"

Mitch frowns at her just the way he looks at me, and I want to jump up and scream, but I just hold Darly close and give Marta a loving look she can't even see. And Mitch shoots.

My ears are humming and the woods are shaking and I hear the second shot ring. I look up and see a few scattered branches fall, but not much green hits the ground. Mitch reloads quick and shoots again so fast we haven't had time to move our hands from our ears. Again he reloads and shoots. He cusses walking in circles, and I can see he would kill these trees if he could for making him walk in the cold and shoot at the wind. He does it again, and again, and Marta has backed up to me now and she crouches against my arm and Darly is holding tight like she thinks the noise alone can rip her away. I look at Marta's green eyes so afraid, and I try to look loving, but my heart is so full of hate I can see she knows it because after looking at me her eyes blink, her mouth jerks, and she holds in a cry. Finally the blasting stops, and I look around and see branches scattered all around us like a storm tore around in a circle and sealed us at its center. I see Mitch mumbling something, and I yell, "What?"

He stares past me and yells, "Pick it up yourself!" as he heads back toward the truck.

We stand, and I try to pull Darly from me so I can see her face, but she presses into me and whimpers, so I hold her and rock her as I walk and look over the ground for my green leaves.

Marta runs ahead. She crouches, stares, runs again, crouches. "I don't see any dead birds," she yells.

"It's a wonder," I say. I bend to pick up my first small branch of this year's mistletoe. I hold it close and stare at those small green-yellow leaves, the white berries that make me think of tiny pearls, and I brush it against my cheek, hold the soft leathery leaves against my skin. I breathe its fresh smell, and I look out at Marta smiling at me just the way I know she sees me smiling at her when I catch her happy in the middle of some quiet thing she loves.

Darly feels my body ease up now, and she leans out and crushes a leaf in her hand and laughs. "Mmmm," she says, and I hug her and pull her hand free.

"Pick up all you can," I say to Marta, and we bend and stand filling our arms fast because we know if Mitch thinks he is missing his football game, he'll drive us out of these woods like runaway slaves. We want to take it all back. We want to fill that house with green. I'll wrap the branches in red yarn and let them dangle so thick with their outdoor smells that my closed little too warm house will feel as wild as these woods, and for little moments when I'm standing there folding clothes, mopping a floor, dusting a shelf, for a second anyway, I can think hard and remember this lake, these sweet rotting leaves, tall trees, and those winter birds who somehow fly fast enough to watch the woods shake and hear the air crash without dying in the noise.

What Happened to Wendell?

The night Wendell Weeks shot his head off, he appeared to Irene in a dream. He sat at the foot of her bed, patted her leg and said, "I'm leaving, Irene. Tell your sister I had to go."

The next morning Irene was so sure it wasn't a dream she asked her sister Lavita what Wendell was doing in the house last night. Lavita just frowned over her strawberry pop-tart and said, "You're dreaming, girl. You know I ain't seen Wendell for weeks."

"You can tell me," Irene said. "How'd you get him in the house without Momma hearing? Did he crawl in a window?"

"I wouldn't let that fool crawl in my window!" Lavita spooned more sugar in her coffee. "What you dreaming about Wendell for?"

Irene stirred her Cheerios. "I don't know," she said.

"Don't bother me with Wendell while I'm eating."

"I always liked him," Irene said.

"Ain't you got something to do?"

Irene got up and went to sit on the porch.

Later that day Lavita got the phone call. Wendell was found

dead on the bathroom floor at the Holiday Inn. He used a twelve-gauge shotgun, pulled the trigger with his toe. When Irene heard about it, all she could think was that Wendell couldn't afford a Holiday Inn. She tried to think of other things, things like he must've been real sad, he must've been scared, but her mind kept saying that he couldn't afford the Holiday Inn.

She didn't want to think about how he came to her room to say good-bye. She didn't want to have to worry about ghosts too. There was enough in the daylight to drive a girl crazy: trying to talk to people who don't listen, trying to be as pretty as Lavita, and then there was her daddy who was gone for good. She kept waiting for the day when a strange man would see her on the street and yell, "That's my girl! Ain't you grown!" Her daddy had been gone so long, Irene wouldn't know him. Her momma burned all his pictures, the clothes he left behind, and even his tools. Irene could remember liking the man, but she couldn't remember exactly why, and it made her sick that something so important could just be gone.

Irene spent a lot of time doing paint-by-number pictures. She knew they were ugly, but she liked watching the little white spaces fill up with color until she had a scene: a sun setting over mountains, a waterfall in the woods, or horses running wild through a field. She liked each painting for about a day. Then she threw them out. Her momma fussed about the waste of good money, but Irene kept painting and throwing them out.

But after Lavita brought Wendell home for a visit, Irene decided she didn't need to paint. At first, she thought he was goofy looking. He was just out of the army and had one of those army haircuts, and his ears stuck out like little wings glued to the sides of his head, but he smiled and seemed friendly enough. Wendell had been in the war, so after talking about the future in construction work, and the high price of cars and homes and everything else, Wendell got around to Viet Nam stories.

He talked as if it had all been a movie. He could say things like dead babies and naked women half-buried in the mud, and he wouldn't flinch. He told how he saw a friend blown to bits right beside him. He had heard a blast, hit the ground, and when he looked up, he saw a leg go flying through the air. "To tell it slows it down, but it happened so fast," he said. "It took one second, and he was gone." After he told each story, he would lean back on the couch and say, "'Nam was hell. Pure hell." Then he'd pop a potato chip in his mouth or take a sip of Coke. Lavita sat next to him and squeezed his hand. Irene looked at the ice in her glass. Her momma rocked and shook her head; then she leaned forward and asked Wendell what he liked to do when he wasn't building houses or gone to war.

His face went round and bright, and he talked about hunting deer in north Georgia mountains, and fishing for bass in Soddy Creek. He said he used to like to camp, but looking at the stars just wasn't the same. Lavita squeezed his arm and said, "You'll learn to like the stars again." Irene watched him look real close at Lavita; she saw his eyes shine and a grin spread across his face.

Irene said, "You want some more Coke, Wendell? Your glass is about empty."

He nodded. "I'm real thirsty." He held out his glass to be re-filled. "Yep," he said. "Everything's going to be all right. Got a job. My hunting gun, my boat—"

"You got a boat?" Irene's momma said.

"Just a twelve-footer. Ain't much. I've been too busy working, but I can't wait to get me a Hula-Popper on the water and coax me a bass out of the weeds."

"A Hula-Popper?" Irene said.

He set his coke down and leaned forward. "Looks like a frog. You jerk it along the top of the water. You give a little tug. It goes plop! You tug again. Plop! Sounds like a frog swimming. Then pow! A bass jumps in the air, grabs it and—"

"I hate fish," Lavita said. "Slimy and they stink. And worms, ooohh!" She shivered and moved closer to Wendell.

He grinned. "I wouldn't let nothing hurt my Lavita."

"I'd like to go fishing sometime," Irene said.

Her momma laughed. "You ain't seen a live fish since you were five years old." She nodded to Wendell. "We'd set her up in a cardboard box by the creek—keep her from running off too easy —and she'd sit all day holding that cane pole, staring at the bob-ber, just waiting. Her daddy hooked the worms for her, took the fish off too."

"When she caught one," Lavita said.

"I caught some. I'd like to go fishing." Irene grabbed a handful of chips.

Wendell said, "I'll take you sometime."

When Wendell left, Irene's momma declared him a neat clean well-behaved young man and said it was a shame such a nice boy went to the other side of the world just to see death and war and blood and legs go flying through the air.

"He wants to marry me," Lavita said.

"Every boy wants to marry you." Her momma smiled as she rinsed out the glasses.

"He loves me a lot," Lavita said. "I'm going to do it."

Irene sat at the kitchen table and watched her momma and Lavita grin and hug and cry. "I like him," she said. "It'll be nice having Wendell around."

Lavita had him at night, but Irene got him for the day. Lavita thought it was just fine that Wendell and Irene got along. She liked to spend her weekends sun-bathing with her friends, or shopping, or doing her nails. She told Irene, "I can't stand that boy breathing down my neck all day, but I don't want him straying too far. Then she winked and said, "When he's with you, I don't have to worry, do I? Fifteen-year-old girl."

"Wendell is my friend," Irene said.

On Saturday mornings Wendell came with his boat tied on top of his banged-up blue Nova, and a cooler full of sandwiches and Nehi grape drinks. The first time Irene saw all the food she laughed and said, "What's a skinny man like you need so much food for?"

"Get hungry on the water," he said. "Let's go."

It took some practice, but Wendell taught Irene how to cast near the shoreline without catching her line in a tree and how to make a Hula-Popper make the right sound. He said she was the best girl fisherman he ever saw.

Then Wendell started acting strange. He got quiet, and he stopped packing sandwiches. All day he'd fish, just smoking cigarettes and drinking grape drink. Irene kept thinking he'd switch to beer, and she knew if he packed beer in the cooler, she wouldn't set foot in the boat. But he kept drinking grape drink, and somehow that worried Irene even more. She had to remember to pack sandwiches in her pocket, or else she'd starve. "You ought to eat," she'd say, but he'd just shake his head, draw on his cigarette, and stare at the end of his line.

Irene could see he was slowly vanishing to nothing but bone. His pants slid low on his hips when he stood to cast. The first time she had seen him take off his shirt in the heat, she couldn't stop looking at his muscles, but now she just saw ribs and a chest bone that made her think of raw chicken. His arms were looking more like an old man's, and even though he was letting his hair grow long, his face seemed to be shrinking, so his ears stuck out all the more.

Irene was also worried about Lavita. The wedding was looking more and more like something bad in the past you didn't talk about. The date kept getting pushed off until Irene's momma gave up and stopped making plans. And Lavita treated Wendell more like a cold that was trying to come on than a fiancée. Sometimes she wouldn't go to the phone when he called. She started crying a lot, and when she came in from a date she went straight to her room.

Irene kept fishing with Wendell because she didn't know what else to do. She knew something was coming. Wendell had always treated her right. But the last time they were fishing Irene was nervous because the night before Lavita had come home with a black eye. Running to her room, Lavita had yelled, "He's a jealous son of a bitch, and I hope he goes to hell!"

Irene banged on Lavita's door and asked, "What happened to Wendell? He used to be so nice!"

Her momma pulled Irene into the kitchen and sat her down. "Hush, girl." she said. "That young man is going crazy." She folded a dish towel on her lap. "He loves her too much," she said. "Got to know where she is every minute. Says he sees her places, says she does trashy things. Lavita's a good girl, you know that. She's just too much for Wendell. They'll never get married now."

"I'm going fishing with him tomorrow," Irene said. "He won't hurt me. Just because Lavita dumps him don't mean I got to lose a friend."

Her momma stood and wiped the table. It was clean, but she kept wiping in circles and looking at the formica as if she expected something would grow out of it if she wiped long enough. "You're right," she said. She sat down and refolded the towel. "Lavita has got to let him go slow. We got to do this real slow. Don't you get him talking about Lavita out in that boat."

Irene nodded. "I'm just gonna talk about fish."

Wendell was quiet the next morning. Irene met him on the front porch as usual, and later when she was stepping in the boat, she asked the usual question, "Are we going to get a monster?"

"Yeah," he said. He started the engine. Usually Irene caught only small bass, or bream. She was used to Wendell getting the big ones, but still, every time she cast out, she wondered if it would be the time a monster bass would strike.

The roar of the engine was too loud to talk, but Irene thought that was fine because she was afraid Wendell would bring up Lavita. She shivered a little in the wind and watched the water spread out in waves behind them.

They had been fishing for about an hour. Irene had some hits, but had caught nothing. She had reached the point where the early excitement of a morning on the water had worn off, when all she could think about was waiting for a hit. At this point she usually ate something, but Wendell was digging in his tackle box and saying he had just the right thing.

"Get me a Hula-Popper," Irene said. She liked Hula-Poppers best because she could see the fish break before the hit instead of just feeling the strange quick tug from under the surface.

"The water ain't right," Wendell said. "Too active." Irene nodded. "Try this," he said. "Bought it last week. A Baby Torpedo." He tossed the lure to Irene. "Watch the hooks!"

Irene carefully caught the lure. She looked at it and twirled the small propeller. "What's it do?"

"Cast it out, reel it in, not too fast, just steady. It looks like a wounded fish on the surface of the water."

"Thought they liked 'em healthy."

"It works," Wendell said.

Irene liked the sound the Torpedo made, a steady whirring splashing noise. She liked the sounds of fishing, the soft click of the reel, the water beating around the aluminum boat, the plopping sound of lures. She thought maybe if Lavita had tried fishing, she and Wendell wouldn't be in such a mess. But she was glad Lavita didn't because it would be hard to fish with three in a boat.

"This sure beats painting," Irene said. Wendell nodded and squinted at his line. She cast the Torpedo in a shady spot near a fallen tree. "Nice," she whispered. She reeled in. Something hit hard, and the rod nearly jumped from her hand. "I got one!"

Wendell reeled in fast and watched her rod bend. "Keep the tip up!"

"I can't." She struggled to keep the tip up and reel in all at once.

"Do it!" Wendell picked up the net and watched the water. "Don't break the line, you bastard." Irene stared at him. She had never heard him swear. "Watch it, Irene, you got a monster!" She tried to reel in, but the line pulled out with a tearing noise. "Fight, you bastard!" Irene saw the bass break, his brown back arched in the light, then he splashed, still fighting, into the water near the fallen tree. "An eight-pounder, at least!" Wendell shrieked. "Get him away from that tree. You'll lose him!"

"I can't," Irene yelled. The rod dipped and shook in her hands. She pulled.

"Not too hard!" Wendell grabbed her arm, and something snapped. Irene's rod jerked back, and she fell into the bottom of the boat. She still held the rod in her hand, but it was so light. There was nothing. She looked up. "What happened?"

Wendell glared and grabbed the rod. He beat it against the water and screamed, "God-damned fish! Caught in a tree! A tree in the god-damned water!" Irene held on to the sides of the boat. She was sitting in a puddle of water. She stared up. "Now he'll die! Got my Torpedo stuck in his mouth and now he'll swim off to the bottom and die." His pounding slowed. "Lost my lure. Lost my fish. Line snapped on a tree." He stopped and looked down at Irene. "You'll get your ass soaking wet."

"It *is* wet," she said. She tried to get up. Wendell bent his knees and dropped to the bottom of the boat.

"It is?" he laughed. He held his head in his hands and looked out at the water. "God-damned stupid-assed bass." He laughed loud and hard. "Stupid fish, thinks he's free." Irene couldn't tell if

Wendell was laughing or crying. "But he's got my Torpedo, and he's going to die." They sat in the bottom of the boat and drifted while Irene watched the water and Wendell leaned back and closed his eyes.

That was the last time Wendell and Irene went fishing. When he took her home, Lavita wouldn't come out of her room. He stood outside her door and yelled, "I'm sorry, Lavita. I guess I love you too much." Lavita wouldn't say a word. But Wendell kept begging. Irene sat in her room and cried until her momma made Wendell leave.

Then Wendell started acting crazy. He called all hours of the night saying if he couldn't have Lavita somebody would die. Sometimes he drove by the house and threw rocks, and once he came into the yard with a gun and shot into the trees. Lavita called the police, but when they got there Wendell was gone.

Then he quit calling. For weeks they didn't hear a word. Irene's momma figured he gave up and moved out of town. Lavita started dating old boyfriends, and Irene went back to her paints.

When Irene had her dream, Lavita didn't want to hear it. And her momma said, "Lord, I hope it don't mean he's coming back." That afternoon when the police called and told how it happened at the Holiday Inn, Lavita dropped to the floor. Wendell had left a note saying that he loved Lavita, but his boat and tackle should go to Irene. He wanted to be burned, not buried. And he wanted Lavita to keep his ashes until the day she died.

At the funeral home, Irene was surprised to see the open coffin. Wendell had aimed the barrel of the gun into his neck, so his face looked normal except for the big dark circles under his eyes. He was even skinnier than Irene remembered. His jaw bone jutted out stiff and strong, not like a face but like something carved, something that would last forever. When Irene looked at his ears still sticking out, a little bit blue, she started to cry. Then Lavita pushed her out of the way so hard she tripped over the flowers and almost fell. She stood back and watched as Lavita wrapped her arms around the coffin and screamed and sobbed and carried on till somebody had to pull her off.

Irene leaned toward her mother and said, "That Lavita's just showing off. She didn't really care."

"Hush!" her momma said.

"She was glad to see him go. Wendell knows I cared. That's why he came to me."

Her momma's face puffed up and got red. "Your sister's in pain and here you brag about communing with the dead. I suppose you like ghosts creeping into your room." People were staring.

"I'm just saying—" Irene whispered.

Her momma got louder. "You'd better get on your knees and pray he don't come back!" She walked off to comfort Lavita. Irene went into the foyer and stared out the window and thought she would give anything to be out in the boat. She was so sleepy she could fall down, and her stomach was beginning to growl. She rested her head against the window and closed her eyes. She had hardly slept since the night Wendell came. She'd lie in bed and stare up at the ceiling, half hoping he'd come, then breaking out in a cold sweat if her eye caught a light or a shadow on the wall. She could hear the soft rise and fall of voices praying in the next room.

She knew they would burn him that night. She could see them pushing the coffin into the furnace, the bright orange, red, and blue flames shooting all around, drawing Wendell in. She saw how the coffin would scorch, bubble, and sizzle in the heat. It would fall apart in seconds, and the flames would eat at Wendell like something starved. He would come to her just when the flames were closing in, he would come to her and make one last sign. He would stand in the corner of her room and burn.

Irene shivered and stepped back from the window. She could hear everyone outside getting into cars. There would be a big dinner at Wendell's aunt's house. His mom and dad had died years ago, so all he had was a brother who came in from Birmingham, some cousins, and this aunt who liked to cook. Irene thought of how everyone would eat until they couldn't move. They'd talk till they got around to the price of things and the dry hot weather. Then they'd go home and watch TV while Wendell burned.

Irene went into the empty room and stood in front of the coffin. She watched the dust float in the sunlight that filtered through the drawn green velvet drapes. The room was cooler with the people gone. She liked the stillness, the darkness, the bittersweet smell of flowers. Wendell lay in the coffin as if he had always been there, as if he belonged in the room, just like the long oak table and the high-backed chairs. Irene could hear the voices in the foyer and knew she had only a minute. She kneeled and whispered, "Wendell. Please don't come to me tonight. You might want to, but you just go on to wherever you've got to go. I'll miss you, but it scares me, Wendell." She heard someone behind her and turned.

"That's my girl," her momma said.

Irene said, "I'm all done now."

Her momma took her arm. "Let's go, honey. It's time to eat."

Wendell never came to Irene again, and in spite of his note and his last wishes, Irene never got the boat. The brother from Birmingham took it saying the note meant nothing and besides Wendell owed him money from years ago. When Irene sat at her desk with her paints, she wondered if she would ever fish again.

Lavita fell in love with a new boyfriend who played golf and sold insurance. Irene thought he was boring and too short to get excited about, but Irene's momma thought he'd do just fine—at least he wasn't the type to get a gun and shoot into trees.

Wendell's ashes started out on Lavita's dresser. Later when Lavita tried to put them in the cellar, her momma moved them to the living-room shelf right over the TV. She said just because time passed was no need to lose respect, and besides, she thought the box was pretty. It was made of heavy brass and had a wreath embossed on the front. Irene said it was the only elegant looking thing in the house and nobody who came in would know it was Wendell.

Sometimes when Irene dusted, she would hold the box and wonder how it could weigh so much. It wasn't that big, maybe eight inches high, but it felt like it weighed twenty pounds or more. It felt solid, like a brick, or a rock. She wondered how one man burned to ashes could be so heavy, a skinny man like Wendell too. Irene thought Wendell would be happy sitting in the living room. She never dreamed that someday someone would steal him.

It happened on the Fourth of July. Irene, Lavita, their momma, and the new boyfriend went to a barbecue and spent the night watching fireworks at Chickamauga Battlefield. When the night wore on and the crowds thinned out, people started talking about

Green Eyes. He was some poor lost Confederate soldier who was still mad about the way the war turned out, so he roamed the fields at night to show anybody who cared to see that he was still fighting and wasn't licked yet. People said if you looked off into the woods, and if you were lucky, you would see a pair of green eyes moving through the trees. Irene didn't want to see Green Eyes, and her momma called it a bunch of bull, so they all got in the car and left before people started getting out their flashlights and walking through the woods.

When Irene's momma walked through the front door, the first thing she noticed was the TV gone. The toaster, Lavita's jewelry box, and her momma's gold watch were stolen too. Lavita stormed around the house, and her boyfriend kept asking why they didn't have insurance, it didn't cost that much. Irene was sitting on the couch when she looked up and saw the empty shelf. "They got Wendell!" She ran across the room and stared at the empty space where the box once sat. "Somebody stole Wendell!"

The policeman said it would be hard to find a box of ashes, it wasn't the kind of thing that somebody could hock. Irene watched him trying not to smile. "Dying's bad enough," she said. "It's a crying shame when a man gets stolen too."

The policeman closed his pad and said, "You're right, miss. What's this world coming to?"

Irene could see that Lavita wasn't bothered the least bit. She just looked like some joke had been played and she couldn't quite figure how it worked. Her new boyfriend said it was probably kids that did it, that they couldn't know what was inside.

"Of course they didn't know," Irene said. "It'd take a jackhammer to get it open."

"They must have thought it was full of coins," the policeman said. "Jewelry. Something of value."

Lavita laughed and said, "Won't they be surprised when they pry that box open and find a bunch of ashes and bones."

Her momma crossed her arms. "I hope Wendell haunts the hell out of them."

Irene moaned. "Now he'll come back for sure."

"That's right," Lavita said, smiling. "Maybe he'll come back and tell you where his ashes are."

Later that night, when the house was dark and quiet, Irene

couldn't sleep. She sat up in the dark and waited for Wendell, who never came.

After a while, Irene's momma put a vase of silk roses where Wendell's ashes used to be, and soon they looked as right and natural on that shelf as anything else that had been sitting around for years. They got a new TV better than the old one. The new toaster worked fine, and Irene's momma got a watch that wasn't gold but kept good time. And it wasn't long before Lavita got a new supply of jewelry to wear.

Irene finally started believing that Wendell was truly gone. She even wondered sometimes if he had truly come to her room the night he died. But she clung to her memory's picture of him patting her leg, looking so sad, and saying bye, she clung to it like a hungry dog clings to a piece of meat with its teeth. There was nothing, nothing left of Wendell but what she remembered, and Irene said she was damned if she would let that get stolen too.

Twirling

In a meadow splattered with Queen Anne's lace and purple thistle, Billy Ruth stood still, stared up, waited for the silver flash of metal to drop into her outstretched hand, ready to twirl, spin, and pitch the shining baton up again to the blue sky. It smacked her palm, and she turned, counted, "One, two, three, up!"

"Billy Ruth, you get in this kitchen," her momma called.

She glanced toward the house, tar-papered to look like brick, brown and peeling in the sun. She pitched again, kept her eye centered on the glancing light, then caught the cool metal in her hand.

"Who ever heard of a one-armed baton twirler?" her momma yelled. "Get in this kitchen right now!"

Her bare feet stirred up red dust as Billy Ruth walked the dirt path to her house. She had worked up a sweat, and the skin under the cast on her arm itched. She rubbed the cast against her side as she walked, and she knew nothing would stop the itch until the cast was sawed off and thrown in the trash. She stood still and rolled the baton between the fingers of her good hand, the right hand.

"Billy Ruth!"

She walked slowly, still waving her fingers, forcing the cool metal to flow like water across her hand.

As she walked into the kitchen, she glanced at her momma, who stood at the stove. "I wouldn't be a one-armed twirler if you didn't make me climb that ladder and wash windows nobody ever sees anyway."

"Don't put your fall on me," her momma said.

"Well, you sure didn't want to climb up there yourself."

"I won't have my house looking like trash. Now eat."

Billy Ruth could smell the whiskey in the glass on the counter across the room. "You gonna eat?" she asked.

"Later." Her momma smiled. "You know me and my midnight snacks."

"Yeah," Billy Ruth said. As she watched her momma set out the fried chicken, sliced tomatoes, and white bread, she remembered walking in the garden with her daddy and watching him bend down to pick a ripe tomato. He would pull a shaker from his hip pocket, and salt the tomato each time he took a bite. Then he would wipe his hands on the large white handkerchief he always carried, and he would move on through the garden. Whenever she told of this memory, her relatives said she was too young to remember. But whether she could see him in the garden from hearing it said, or from standing there next to him and looking up at the tall dark man who ate fresh whole tomatoes as neatly as a deer picking bark off a tree, whether she witnessed it, or imagined it, she knew it was true.

Billy Ruth looked at the food laid out in front of her. "I don't know why you cook," she said as she got up from the table. "You don't eat, and I can't."

"What you mean you can't eat?"

"Fat. I'm getting fat. See." With her good hand she pulled at the flesh on her thigh. Then quickly she got up and walked to the back door and stood looking out the screen.

"You ain't fat," her momma said. "It's that boy in the green truck that's got you skimping on food." Billy Ruth listened to the sounds of clinking ice, the quiet sound of pouring whiskey, the pop and fizz of a Coke being opened. "If you don't like big, hot suppers, blame it on that daddy of yours. He's the one that said, 'If you ever neglect my baby, I'll come back and haunt the hell out of you!' What kind of thing is that for a dying man to say?" She pointed at Billy Ruth with the hand that held the drink. "You know what he said."

"I know."

She kept pointing. "New shoes every season. Clean clothes, and hot suppers every day. You know how he was. Do you have any idea how hard it is to buy new shoes every time the leaves change?"

"I know," Billy Ruth said. She had heard it every season. When she saw the leaves sprouting green or changing bright colors, she knew that any day her momma would grab her arm and say, "Let's go." Whether she needed them or wanted them, she had to have new shoes.

"He died in October, you know."

"I know." Billy Ruth stared out through the screen. Her mother was standing just behind her shoulder, and Billy Ruth could smell her warm sour breath when she spoke.

"He had this deadly fear of cold. 'Cause when he was a kid he lost those three toes. Out ice skating, and you know boys, they'll skate till their legs fall off. Don't feel the cold, the wind, the tired, nothing. He always did walk a little funny after losing them toes. Remember how he walked?" Billy Ruth nodded. "It does something to a man, you know, to walk a little funny. I guess it's a wonder he wasn't nutty as a fruitcake. Remember how he'd wear those hats, scarves, two sweaters, plus a coat, and three pair of thick socks. I'd have to buy his shoes two sizes too big to get all that wool in. He hated winter like he knew it would kill him. Nobody even thought about poison kidneys killing a man so handsome and big as Avery." She touched Billy Ruth's arm. "It's not like something you can bundle up and keep from the cold."

She stepped back and walked across the kitchen. "You'd better eat."

"I'm not hungry," Billy Ruth said. She watched her momma pull apart a chick wing, take a bite, then throw it in the trash.

"Love." Her momma grinned. "You girls think it's love when you can't eat, but you're just afraid ol' green truck is gonna think you're fat and find somebody new."

"His name is Tack Caldwell."

"How would I know?" All I ever seen is a green truck parked down the road."

"How's the dog doing?" Billy Ruth asked as she walked across the room.

"Just about dead. I've told you about dragging things home."

In the corner of the kitchen, Billy Ruth had set up a box filled with old clothes as a bed for the puppy she had found at the dump. It lay there and stared up blankly as she reached down and touched his head with the tip of her finger. "Looks like he ain't moved all day," she said.

Her momma was clearing the table. "He stinks like he's dead and don't know it yet."

Billy Ruth looked in the trash and pulled out a piece of the chicken wing. She held it under the puppy's nose. "Come on pup. Don't that smell good?" The dog stared past her.

"If he don't like my fried chicken, he's dead for sure," her momma said.

"Shut up," Billy Ruth said as she stood up. "I wish you'd quit saying death like it's your favorite word."

"Didn't know you were so sensitive. That broken wrist hurt your head too?" She continued clearing the counter. Billy Ruth sat and watched her. "It's your daddy dying that got you shy on death," her momma said. After what your aunt Lucy did, it's no wonder. Enough to make anybody scared of death for life. It ain't your fault, honey."

Billy Ruth got up and looked in the refrigerator. "I'm going to see if that dog will eat some scrambled eggs," she said. Her momma was finally quiet, and as Billy Ruth stood at the stove and stirred the eggs, she remembered how her daddy lay in a coffin of deep blue satin and dark wood. The colors made his skin seem blue, almost black where he wrinkled. Seeing that dark face, lips painted like old rubber, how could anyone believe that when he laughed you could feel the air stir as he gasped for breath and laughed harder still?

She had worn a pink dress so stiff with starch and three crinolines that it swayed like a bell when she pressed her hands on either side. Someone had suddenly lifted her by the waist and held her over the dark man in the coffin. "Kiss him good-bye," someone said. "Kiss your daddy bye." She was pushed to his face, and she kissed. Then she fought free and stroked her lips that burned and peeled for days. Then her hair fell out. "Nerves," someone said. Then she began burying her dolls, just to dig them up, wash them off, and bury them again.

She heard her momma shaking the ice in her drink and saw that the eggs were drying out in the pan. She scraped them into an old margarine cup and placed them in front of the dog. He blinked once and continued to stare. Billy Ruth stood up and put the frying pan in the sink. "People ought to be shot for dumping a dog like that. He could have been a good hunting dog some day. You can tell he's part beagle." Her momma shook the ice in her glass. "Tack could've used a good hunting dog," Billy Ruth said as she bent down and picked up the bowl of eggs and dumped them into the trash.

Her momma watched her. "I never did like hunting. Your daddy didn't either. Not since Buddy Haskins got shot for a deer. Your daddy wouldn't touch deer meat after Buddy died. Happens all the time when you get too many men shooting off guns in the woods. They say those bullets can travel five miles before they drop—if nothing gets in their way. For five miles that bullet can whiz straight through the air as long as it don't hit a tree, a rock, a mountain, or a man. It's a wonder more men don't die with those bullets whizzing around."

"Tack don't use those five-mile bullets," Billy Ruth said. "He hardly ever goes for something big."

Her momma was mixing another drink. "What about baton twirlers, I hear they get mighty big for their britches sometimes."

"I'm not a baton twirler. I just do it to get out of the house."

"Shit, honey, you're out there every chance you get."

"Guess I need to get out a lot," Billy Ruth said. She picked up her baton from the table and walked toward the door. "Got to go practice before it gets dark." She pushed on the screen and went out.

She could feel autumn coming in the cool breeze. It had been one of those September days when the bees hovered and sweat ran as if the August heat were having its last stand, but she could smell the clean air of coming October nights as she watched the sun go down between slate blue mountains. Night sounds were just beginning, and the starlings, thick as leaves in the silver maple, filled the yard with their high squeaking noise. She walked toward her quiet spot to pitch the baton. She made it spin and flash faintly silver in the growing dark. It was harder with one hand, but she worked, pitched, and turned with such effort that she didn't see the red dirt going gray in the dim light. She didn't hear the starlings' banter, or the crickets winding up to a frenzied noise that could make a half acre of weeds ten miles from anywhere sound full with too much life.

She heard Tack's truck before she saw it. She heard the tires spinning gravel as he climbed the hill, then the high creaking sound of brakes, and finally the rumbling grinding sounds of the engine as it came to a halt.

As if she hadn't heard him, she kept spinning and marching in circles with her knees high, bare toes pointed, and her eyes fixed on a vague point directly in front of her face. Finally she missed a beat, and the baton dropped to the ground, bounced and banged against her thigh.

"Not bad for a cripple," Tack yelled from the truck.

Smiling she ran toward him. Then she stepped up on the running board and leaned in to be kissed.

"Get in," he said.

She leaned over and looked into the back of the truck. "What's all this?"

"Copper wire. Aluminum. Sheet metal. Good money in junk if you know what sells." He reached out and squeezed her waist. "Bet I could get a dime for that baton of yours."

"Worth more than that," Billy Ruth said.

"Looks like it's worth about a nickel to me."

She threw it behind her back and turned to watch it bounce into the weeds. "Go get it if you want to."

"That ain't what I want."

She looked into his face and leaned back as she supported her weight with one hand gripping the door handle. "What do you want, Tack Caldwell?" she said. "Huh?"

"I think you got an idea." He reached for her again, but she jumped down and walked into the weeds to get her baton.

He watched her. "When you gonna grow up, Billy Ruth?"

She stepped back onto the running board and shrugged. Then she shook her head and let her hair slap his face.

"Get in this truck, girl," he said. She smiled and ran around the truck to climb into the passenger's seat. Tack reached into a small grocery bag. "I brought you something."

"Shrimp cocktail!" She moved close beside him and kissed his cheek. "I only have two dozen shrimp cocktail glasses saved back in my room."

He handed her one of the plastic spoons he kept in the glove compartment and watched as she dug into the red sauce. "What you gonna do with them little glasses? It's not like they hold enough to drink." He pulled a magnetized bottle opener from the dashboard and opened his grape drink.

"Maybe I'll make a parfait," she said.

"You don't even know what a parfait is."

"It's something you make with Jello," Billy Ruth said. Then she shoved a large spoonful of shrimp into her mouth.

Tack watched her chew as she looked for more shrimp. "When we gonna do it, Billy Ruth?"

"What? Make a parfait?"

"Yeah," he said. He watched her dig out the last piece of shrimp, and then he grabbed her hand and pulled the spoon to his mouth. He opened wide, and then clamped his mouth down on the spoon. He grinned as he swallowed her last bite.

"Didn't your momma teach you no manners?" He pulled his shirttail out of his jeans and wiped his mouth and shook his head.

She jabbed his flat stomach with her fist and yelled, "How do you stay so skinny, boy?"

"I work it off. You know."

"Sure," she said.

"Ought to try it sometime." He pinched a tiny roll of flesh at her side.

"Thanks for the shrimp, Tack. But I got to get in the house and check on that dog." Tack tilted up his soda bottle and in several long hard swallows emptied it. "How's he doing?" he said as he wiped his mouth with the back of his hand.

"Just about dead. I'm waiting until it's over so I can bury it in the back yard.

"It's just like you to go to the trouble to bury something somebody else threw in the dump. When you gonna quit fussing over other people's trash?"

"I heard you can make good money on junk." Billy Ruth leaned out the window and scraped the remaining cocktail sauce onto the ground. "Besides," she grinned back at him, "I've heard more than one person call you trash."

"That's because I am." He grabbed her and shoved his hand between her legs.

"Watch my arm, Tack!" she yelled. Then she stopped struggling because she knew one more ounce of pressure would cause pain, and she refused to let him hurt her.

"I want this," he said. "It ain't like you never done it before."

"You think you know me?" She looked out the window and tried not to feel the weight of his hand.

"I know enough." He pushed her hair away from her face. "I want it," he said softly, "and I don't want to have to fight you for it."

"Okay, Tack. Okay," she said.

"Good." Suddenly he let go of her and sat straight up behind the steering wheel. She watched as he took a piece of copper wire from off the dashboard and pulled a small knife from his pocket. He cut away the plastic coating from one end of the wire, then wound the bright copper around the tip of his knife. Slowly he pulled the wire free from the plastic. Then he twisted it into a small bracelet and slipped it over Billy Ruth's hand. "There," he said. "Now what you gonna do?" He released her and sat back.

Billy Ruth looked out at the fading colors of the field as the sun began to disappear behind the mountains. The flowering weeds shivered on brittle stalks as the night breeze stirred. Her house looked still and dark as a rock. She thought her momma had turned out all the lights so she could peer out the window without being seen, but then she remembered it was time for her momma's favorite comedy show. Billy Ruth rolled down her window and listened. Hearing the faint grating sound of laughter from the TV, she shook her head. "Momma's comedy shows. They scream and laugh so loud it hurts, and Momma sits there and goes to sleep. She can't sleep at night in the quiet. It's like she needs that awful laughing to fill the house before she can let her eyes close."

"I hate that shit," Tack said.

"Yeah."

He turned to her. "So what do you say, girl?"

"You think that dog I found is dead yet?"

"Prob'ly." Tack gently picked up her arm, and he kissed just where the cast covered her wrist. "Still hurt?"

"Not much," she said.

"So, baby. It's dark as dirt, and the crickets are going loud enough to drown out laughing or screaming or anything else that might happen out here."

She listened to the sounds in the breeze. Still looking out at the dark, she said, "When my daddy died I wore a pink satin dress that stood out so full they said I looked like a rose. Funny how you remember things."

When she looked back at Tack, she didn't see his face as he pressed down on top of her and covered her mouth with his own. She felt her body sink deep into the seat when his weight pressed down on her as if his body could push out all light, all breath, the crickets, the laughter, and the trees shivering in the breeze around them. She wanted to hide in the darkness he made, but she felt him pulling at her shorts as if his movements were a secret she couldn't possibly know.

"Okay, Tack, stop," she said. "I'm doing this. I won't let you do this to me." And with every muscle she could strain for, she threw herself at him. Wrapping arms and legs around him, pushing all of herself against him, she forced every nerve to feel each sensation like bright needles touching her skin. She pushed herself forward to him with all her strength, and she felt the silver flashing power of her own force in the dark.

Trailer Fire

Jacob watched the green reeds rush, the brown stalks shake as he drifted down the channel. A black crow rose, flapped wide wings and sank to the marsh grass rippling in the breeze. Jacob cast long and smooth. The torpedo lure sailed through the air, sank inches from the shore where he hoped the bass hid.

"It is there," Rita said. He looked up, saw her sitting at the bow of the boat, and he knew he was dreaming. She pointed to the water, and he looked, saw the dark fin of a bass break water just beyond where he had dropped his lure. He tried to imagine the mind of a fish. She had taught him that, how to let his mind go to the muddy river bottom, where the fins of a fish stirred up silt and algae in brown spirals. "Cast again," she said. And he did, knowing she knew about fish. She had always caught the most fish. He wanted to turn to her, say, "Rita. How did you come back?" He wanted to jump across the boat, get close enough so she would touch with that hand of hers, that hand that moved once across his back in slow light circles. "Cast," she said. And he did, trying to put his mind in the mind of that fish down there, thought, "But a fish can't think, Rita." But she would have said, "How do you know?" He cast, thinking, "How do you know?" afraid to look up, afraid if he looked she would be gone. So he stared at the gray water, watched the line move, listened to the click of the reel.

The crow called loud like metal ripping just behind his head. The sound tore his ears, shook his spine, and the boat, Rita, the water, were gone. He ground his teeth in the noise. He shook and woke to the sound of the alarm. Fire. His hand reached for the jackboots beside his bed, while his eyes tried to open.

"Keep moving," he said. "You can do this in your sleep." The metallic whine shook the air and pounded his body with sound. He knew the shock was enough to kill a man, the yank from deep sleep, the grinding noise, the rush, clutching for jackboots, gloves, and gear.

Jacob moved down the hall with the others. He felt like a fish in strong current. Rita would like that. Rita. He saw the men had found their gear and their places on the engine already running.

It was dark, but Jacob knew any minute the eastern sky would lighten. The engine pulled them, and he sat beside the driver who stared at the road as if it could rise and unwind, shake them into the trees.

He looked back at the men in their places. They had automatically reached behind their shoulders and slipped on air tanks, found the masks they hoped they wouldn't need. "They are good men," he thought. "Fear on hold. Just where it should be." They looked awake and ready, and just a little bored as the engine pulled them down empty streets. "Fear on hold. Right behind the eyes."

His heart found its normal rhythm as they rode toward the college. He knew it would be a false alarm. He sat back and tried to slip for a minute back into his dream. Rita. Rita had said, "Cast. It is there," and she was laughing. Laughing like a girl, like Molly, Molly so much like her mother, to look at her made his teeth hurt, made him want to grab her into his arms, pull her to his chest and cry. Rita would have said, "Do it, Jacob. It won't kill you to show a little love sometime." Rita. Just once he wished he had touched her when she didn't ask him to.

They made the turn for the college, and he knew it would be a false alarm. The ride was almost over, and they didn't smell smoke yet. It was smoke that always sent their hearts pounding. When they smelled it, they always leaned forward, eyes widened, and their fingers—he'd seen them—always reached for something, a handle, a lever, a seat cover, their own knees, something. When they smelled smoke they always looked for something to hold.

Jacob's hand stretched, closed into a fist at his side. He forced his fingers to relax, but still they curled in toward his palm. "You always look like you're ready to jump into a fight," Rita had said. She would laugh, knock his chest with a light tap of her hand, say "Bulldog."

He could see her lying there in the hospital, her once soft body all bones, her face thin and dry as old paper, and her mouth puckered tight, almost like a fish, not Rita, not the woman with the green eyes that flashed like silver, with the hair blowing across his throat when they rode close in his pickup truck with the windows rolled all the way down. He thought, "But I'm not a bulldog." He could hear her laughing. "God damn, Rita, why'd you ever love me?"

Six months wasn't enough to recover from a dying that came so fast, a dying that left him with an empty house, with nothing but the noise of the refrigerator. At the funeral someone said, so many said, "At least you have a daughter to console you." Yes he did, that was something, even though her eyes flashed so like her mother's that when he looked at her he felt something in his bones break.

They took another turn, and Jacob saw the college dorm's sharp lines against the night, the white light in the stairwells glowing, and the circle of girls standing under the trees, waiting. Not a hint of smoke in the air. He looked back at the men, nodded. Yes, thank god, it was a false alarm. He thought, "Stupid girls. They ought to see a real fire sometime." He wanted to shut them all up in a burning building just for a second, put them near the heat and let them fight the smoke just so they would see.

Jacob watched the men keep their faces blank as they stepped from the engine, grabbed the gear, and climbed the stairwells. They would search the building's corners for a flame they knew wasn't there. He saw the sky going purple. "This won't take long," he thought, and he watched the girls under the trees with their arms crossed, staring up almost as if they wished the building would suddenly flash and explode.

The men returned and he gave the sign to the security man who then nodded to someone, and they all stood together, shook their heads, and watched the girls go back inside. The girls didn't look at his men. Jacob was surprised they didn't joke a little with the men in their uniforms, battle gear, equipment. He had always thought they were impressed by things like uniforms. But these girls were more like little girls in their houseshoes and robes, and their hair in curlers, some holding bags of chips, old teddy bears. They didn't know a god-damned thing. These girls were nothing like Molly.

He looked at the sky, thought of Molly sleeping now. She'd be cooking breakfast for him in a few hours. She had called him. She was always calling to say, "Let's go fishing. Let's get supper. Let me cook you breakfast," as if she could fill the gap between him and Rita. "Well, you can't," he thought. He wanted to scream at her sometimes, sometimes he just wanted to scream. He shook his head at the campus police chief as the last of the girls went inside. They crossed their arms and watched the door close.

The men climbed back on the engine and grinned at each other. They talked about the girls in their short nightgowns. Jacob was proud of his men. At the scene they acted as if they just saw a job to be done, but Jacob knew they didn't miss a glimpse of smooth leg in the light.

When Jacob saw young women, he saw only daughters. He wouldn't want his daughter standing in the dark, staring at a cold building while young men in jackboots and flame-retardant clothes passed by looking for a flame and looking instead at the shape of a leg. Jacob climbed into the engine and couldn't help smiling. It was morning. No smoke. No fire. Just morning, and Molly was cooking breakfast, yes, he would see Molly soon.

Jacob was happy as he turned down the narrow dirt road leading to Molly's house. "I got a good truck," he thought. It was a new truck, a black Toyota, four-wheel drive. "A good truck," he said as he gripped the steering wheel. Molly had made him buy it. After Rita died, she told him he needed something new. Rita had always wanted him to get a new truck. "You need a new truck," she had said. "You need a new truck," Molly said. Just like her mother, she always hid a want with the word "need."

Now he saw her log cabin there under the trees. She called it a house, but he thought of it as a toy, as if she were still a girl with little toy dishes and plastic food painted to look real.

He parked the truck under the sycamore and saw Molly come out and stand on the porch. He couldn't believe he had anything to do with the making of something so pretty. He watched the way she tilted her head to one side, smiled, and waved her hand with one quick move, and he thought, "There she is. Rita." His heart pounded. He heard her say, "Hey, old man. You hungry this morning?"

He nodded and stepped out of the truck. He listened to the jays squawk in the trees and smelled bacon cooking as he stepped up on the porch and met her in the doorway where she handed him the coffee already milky and sweet.

"I got to get my biscuits out," she said.

He followed her into the kitchen and sat at the table. He looked up at a map of the world stretched across the wall. "Think global," Molly always said. She said the map kept her mindful of the world. Just like Rita, she was always thinking about other countries, things happening in places no one ever heard of.

Jacob stared at the map, a flat picture of the world. "Like a squashed orange," he thought. He looked at the bright colors, shades of green, yellow, purple, orange. The map made the world look simple. Everything was arranged. Jacob turned to Molly. "I never liked maps," he said. "Make you think if you follow a little black line, the road will take you where you want to go."

"Maps can't tell you everything," she said.

"Maps lie," he said. "Make you think everything's right where it ought to be." Rita would have reached for him then, would have said, "But it is, Jacob. You're here. I'm here. We've got a healthy girl sleeping in her room. It's all right where it ought to be." She was always talking like that. He felt the old scream rising, thought, "No! You're gone. Rita. Nothing in the whole damned world is right. Not a god-damned thing!"

Molly looked at him and shook her head. She turned toward the door, said, "Let's eat." And he followed her outside to the table under the trees.

Jacob ate quickly. He tried to slow down, but he always ate quickly. He watched Molly, who ate like her mother, held her fork with one hand while she kept the other hand neatly in her lap.

He was staring, so he bent to his plate, put some jelly on his biscuit, tried not to think of Rita, Molly, Rita. He remembered the way Rita could hold her so sure in her long hands, and the way his own hands shook as if Molly were made of Jello that could just slide through his fingers. "Just hold on to her," Rita had said. "She won't go anywhere as long as you don't let go." Jacob thought, "Liar."

He looked again at Molly. Her earrings didn't match. They were both brass dangling shapes that glittered in the sun, but they were different shapes, and one had purple beads. "Your earrings don't match," he said.

She grinned. "They're not supposed to."

He wanted to ask why, but he didn't. "It's probably a statement," he thought. Lately with her, everything was a statement. "You look happy," he said.

"I am." She buttered another biscuit.

He loved the way she ate. He thought, "A healthy girl." That's what the nurse had said. "You've got a healthy girl, Mr. Jenkins."

She looked up. "Want to do some fishing? I hear the trout are running good."

"No," he said, thinking, "Not yet." He couldn't go fishing with Molly. She'd been saying it for months. "We need a fishing trip." But no, he fished with Rita or he fished alone. He wanted to shake her sometimes, yell, "No, Molly, you can't do that." Rita knew about fish. He wanted Rita. She always knew where the fish hid. "It is there," she had said. He held his cup out to Molly. "You got more coffee?" he said.

He heard the sound of an engine coming down the dirt road, spinning gravel, the driver coming too fast. He sat up, heard music shake the trees, rock and roll.

"That's Derek," Molly said. Jacob thought, "Great, the new boyfriend. Where in the hell did you get a name like Derek?" He looked out at the red truck, the same model as his. Molly had taken him to the lot, pointed to the truck said, "There it is. That's the truck for you." Now he knew why. Derek. He watched as the tall wiry guy with a red scarf tied over his head jumped from the truck, thought, "Looks like a god-damned gypsy." The kid held out his hand to shake like a banker, said, "I'm Derek. I've been hoping to meet you."

Molly was standing, holding Jacob's cup, but she was grinning at the guy with the handkerchief on his head like he was some kind of fairy that just popped out of the trees. "You hungry?" she said.

"Starved," he said. He sat at the table, looked straight at Jacob and grinned. "She's a great cook, but she makes me do the dishes. She make you do dishes?"

Jacob looked up at Molly, but she turned away. She was grinning, trying not to. He knew that old guilty drop of the head, knew she was sleeping with this kid with his head in a handkerchief. "Be nice," he thought. That's what Rita always said. "Be nice, Jacob." He watched Molly walk away, heard her say, "I'll get you a plate."

Jacob watched Derek settle back into Molly's chair. His hair was thick and waved like it wanted to fly out from under the red handkerchief. Jacob thought, "Funny looking, but he's not a hippie. Looks too smart. Probably an artist. Molly always liked those arty types." He told himself he would be careful of what he said because the young arty types listened. And they argued. "No bullshit about the weather with this one."

He watched Derek finish off Molly's biscuit. "I'm starved," he said.

"I know," Jacob thought as he pulled his plate closer to his side of the table and picked up his fork. His plate was empty, so he put down his fork and picked up his napkin and leaned over the table. "You an artist?"

Derek laughed. "No, I'm a cartographer." Jacob didn't see what was so funny, but he sat back and watched this kid with a handkerchief on his head take a sip of Molly's juice. "I make maps," the kid said.

"I know what a cartographer is," Jacob said. His voice didn't sound friendly, so he smiled. "You don't look old enough for a job like that."

"I've heard that before," Derek said.

Jacob looked toward the door and wondered why Molly was taking so long. "How do you make maps?"

"I go up in planes, take pictures, then come back down and try to put what I saw in flat little lines on a blank page. Measuring a mountain is harder than you'd think," he said. "Something gets lost in translation."

Jacob nodded. "Exactly," he said. "I don't like maps."

"Molly does." Derek looked toward the kitchen.

Jacob said, "Maps would be all right if they didn't lie sometimes." He had a feeling he was talking about something he didn't know.

Molly brought out a tray with Derek's plate, juice, and more coffee. Jacob watched him eat. He saw that Molly had arranged the plate just as she did for him, the biscuits open, one buttered with jelly on the side, one covered in gravy, sliced tomato banked to the side so the juice wouldn't run in the eggs. "I hear the cook's pretty good," he said. "You eat here often?"

"Every chance I get," Derek said, smiling.

Jacob stood. "I'm getting a glass of water. Want anything?"

Derek was chewing. "Nope," Molly said. "We're just fine."

Jacob stepped inside the kitchen and realized he was sweating. He was losing Molly. She was slipping through his hands just as he knew she would, just as Rita had, Rita who lied, who said, "She's not going anywhere as long as you hold on." He sat at the table and looked around at Molly's house. It was filled with the things her mother left her. The bright dishes that were cheap in the fifties but worth something now. He saw the quilt his mother made. He looked at pictures arranged above bookshelves, photographs of his family, Rita's family, old cousins, friends. Molly loved to frame the old pictures. Jacob thought that women were much better at keeping the past around them. In his own house he felt surrounded by appliances.

He finished his water and wiped his forehead with a paper towel. He heard them laughing outside. Yes, Molly was already gone. He could tell by the way she grinned at that kid in the handkerchief, that kid who flew in airplanes, who drove a red Toyota truck just like his own. He went to the door and looked out. They had their arms around each other, and Derek leaned as if offering something, a secret, a kiss, something Molly wanted, he could tell by the laughing.

Jacob wished just once he had held Rita like that, under trees somewhere laughing, instead of the way he held her that last morning in the hospital with her arm thin and dry as a stick when he finally reached to touch her without her asking, when it was too late to hold her in the world, too late to hold her in his arms, too late for living. "I'm sorry," the nurse said. "Your wife is gone." So he walked around and around that hospital room, until finally Molly grabbed his arm, said, "Daddy, stop, please." So he stopped at the window, stared out, seeing nothing but a gray morning fog spread over the city. Rita was gone, and Molly was crying, and he was staring out at the city, not seeing a thing.

He turned and looked at the map. He saw the words Fiji, Hong Kong, Kuwait, Trinidad, and felt as if he were in another country and would never speak the language. He heard them talking now, that Derek talking so easy, them both talking and laughing the way women do. How the hell did they do it? He stared at the map and thought he wanted to be in his living room.

He took a deep breath and stepped outside. "I'm going," he said, as he headed for the truck.

Molly stood and followed him. "What's wrong?"

"Nothing," he said. He kept his eyes on the truck.

"We could go fishing," she said. "Derek's leaving soon. We need to go fishing. Come on, Dad. I know you need to go fish."

He got in his truck, slammed the door, said, "You don't know a god-damned thing."

She jumped back and stared as if she'd been slapped. He thought, "Why did you say that?" He wanted to say, "I'm sorry, baby," but she was already gone, she was walking away. He started the engine. He needed to be home, in his house, in his chair. He wanted to open a beer, turn on the TV. He watched that kid in the handkerchief hold his daughter, thought, "To hell with you, Derek! To hell with you, Molly. To hell with your truck and your maps, to hell with every god-damned thing." He shoved the truck in gear and headed down the dirt road to the highway that would take him home.

Jacob was awake when the fire alarm rang. He was staring up at the dark ceiling wondering how he would ever talk to Molly. She hadn't called in two days. She was stubborn, god damn it, that was one thing she didn't get from Rita. He was wide awake. He was staring at the ceiling, pounding his fist into the mattress when the alarm screamed.

He stepped in his jackboots and moved down the hall. He heard "trailer fire," the words moving through the air like a bad odor. The men hated trailers. They smoked. They melted. You couldn't guess the action of a trailer. They smoldered, then without warning they could explode.

The siren wailed as the engine pulled them through the night. Jacob looked straight ahead and watched the red taillights of cars braking, pulling over to let the engine through.

They turned onto a dark road, passed the gravel pit, and headed straight for the trailer park. Jacob had been there. He hated the place. Too many kids, too many poor, in too many small places. As they came up on the curve where he knew there was a hydrant, he had to make the hard choice: tell the men to lay a line from the hydrant or trust there was enough water in the tank on the engine. They took the turn, kept moving, and Jacob kept his mouth shut. He'd trust the tank. He'd radio the second engine to lay a line if he saw the need, but he knew the tank would be plenty.

He saw the trailers sitting under skinny trees, fire bombs ready to explode. He smelled the smoke. He gripped his knee and leaned forward. Not a flame in sight. "A smoker," he thought. A smoker could be deadly with very little flame. He saw the women standing with their arms crossed under the trees, kids standing in nightgowns, and men waving their arms, shirtless in the night air, wearing nothing but jeans.

Jacob stepped off the engine and told the men to pull the booster line, thinking the small hose should be plenty. They got the line ready and waited for his signal to go in. He could feel the heat thirty yards back as he led the way toward the trailer. He heard a woman yell, "Somebody's in there!" They always screamed that. Even when it was empty someone always screamed.

He stepped up to the door, felt for the heat. It was hot but not too hot. The door was always the trick. He'd seen a man die once when the open door made a backdraft, when he saw the whole thing explode. He felt the door again. Not too hot. He stepped back, gritted his teeth, grabbed the handle and pushed the door open. Black smoke billowed out.

He gripped the hose and stepped inside. The heat hit him like a wall. "An oven," he thought. "400 degrees at least." The smoke was black and he couldn't see a thing. He dropped to his knees. They would have to crawl. The lights, the noise, and the action of the outside were blotted out. He saw nothing, heard nothing but the rasping sound of men breathing through tanks and the distant cracking popping sound of something burning somewhere. He moved forward in the heat. He moved slowly with the men just behind as they all crawled toward the fire.

He stretched his eyes wide, as he always did, knowing it was useless, knowing in a trailer fire you were always blind. He wanted to move his hands to his face to see if his eyes were open, but the mask and the gloves and the heat blocked everything. "I can't see you, but I hear you, boys," he yelled. It was important to talk to the men when they were blind. They needed to hear a human noise. "I hear you breathing," he said. "Keep your hand on the hose. Just hang on, we're moving in."

He hoped he wouldn't crawl over a body. He remembered the fire in the warehouse. When the smoke had cleared, he looked down and saw he was standing in the middle of a man's chest. Now he moved carefully forward. He heard the ladder crew behind him, searching. They usually found the bodies near the door, then pulled them out fast to see if anyone could be revived. He heard the men search, heard the loud hum of ventilation fans. "Get this damned smoke cleared," he said. He didn't know if he was speaking out loud or to himself. The darkness got hotter. They were getting close.

"Hold the line," he yelled. "Please hold the line," he thought. He remembered when a new man had let go and gotten lost and stood in the blackness screaming until men had found him by following his voice. When they got him out, he threw off his gear and ran away screaming, "I ain't gonna die in someone else's fire."

To the right Jacob felt the source of the heat. He looked up and saw the dull glow of flames. "Got the fire," he said. "Steady boys." He stood, and the men followed. The hose jerked in his hands and the water roared as they blasted the walls, the ceiling, the floor. The force of air and heat and water made a wind that beat against them like a storm. They stood steady and fought for balance. In a few minutes the flames were out.

Jacob told the men to back up and let the smoke clear. He wanted to get outside, make his report to the chief, and breathe the cool night air. Slowly they backed out the narrow dark hall, still tricky with unknown corners, strange objects strewn across the floor.

Finally outside, the men jerked off their masks for a breath of real air. Jacob looked down and saw a young woman stretched out, twisted, half naked on the ground. He saw the muscled calves, the bare feet, the worn cotton robe, and he thought, "Someone's daughter."

He moved closer. The ambulance crew stood around her. Her head was tipped back, chin tilted up, eyes wide open like red wounds. Then he saw the baby, with its blackened diaper wrinkled around fat thighs that should be kicking, but the infant was still. Jacob couldn't tell if it was a boy or girl. It looked peaceful. He hoped it had drifted away quietly in the hot black clouds.

One of the men retched behind him, and Jacob thought the sight should make him retch too, but it didn't. He stared. He was numb, thinking someone's daughter, someone's child. The woman could have been one of those college girls he saw standing safe and bored in the night. But this girl never went to college. This girl lived and died in a trailer. She lay there stretched out, blackened, ugly, twisted, stiff.

Her fists were clenched, and her arms crossed over her chest. One fist was covered in brown dried blood. Jacob's stomach rolled. He had seen the bloody fist before, a sign of someone trying to beat her way through a wall. She had pounded and pounded and never broke through.

The search crew said they found her in the kitchen. She must have come down the hall in the dark, somehow missed the door and went straight in the kitchen where she must have turned round and round looking for her way out.

Jacob went back inside. He moved to the blackened tiny closet of a room. He saw the charred mattress that sat there crisp and black. He saw another body, clothes burned off, a woman's body shriveled, black like a mummy, peaceful as if the woman never knew what she had started when she drifted off.

"God damn," Jacob whispered. He moved down the hall and saw the blood marks on the kitchen wall, splotches of dried blood where the first woman pounded her fist. She had been standing two feet from the door. She must have turned round and round in the black cloud that sat in the trailer like a huge furred beast sucking up air. He looked at the plants, the apples on the table, the print of a mountain landscape. It all looked dead. The black beast had moved out the door and drifted into the night, where its sharp odor would cause someone to lift his head, smell the air and say something is burning somewhere.

Jacob thought no one should die pounding on a wall. He hurried outside. The men stood whispering. They always whispered around the dead. Jacob wanted to scream.

He decided the chief could wait. He walked straight out to the dirt road. He kept walking until he found a clearing where he could look up at the sky. He remembered that when Molly was a girl he liked to take her out at night to show her the stars, and all she had wanted to do was chase fireflies. He could see her hands reach, hear her laughter when she held something.

He went back to the engine to wait for the chief. He looked at his hands. They were black. It always happened, the black smoke got under his clothes, in his eyes, ears, nose, skin.

He watched the ambulance crew lift the body bags and slide them into the back of a white truck. The younger attendant slammed the door, then looked at the ground. The older attendant, a big man, reached and held his shoulder. They leaned into each other for an instant, one man holding the other's shoulder. Then quickly they released. Jacob felt his eyes burn.

He looked back at his own men. One held his helmet in his lap and stared. Another man looked at his hands. The newest man leaned back with his eyes closed while his hands gripped his knees as if his legs were trying to run away. The men weren't talking, weren't touching. Jacob wanted to hold them all. Rita would think like that. He remembered Rita in the dream, Rita smiling, pointing at the gray water. "It is there."

He could hear her laughing that quick sharp sound whenever she hooked a fish. She always yanked it up with a little burst of laughing as she gripped the rod, cranked the reel. Molly would fish like that. He could hear Molly laughing. She had said, "We need to fish." She had said it just like Rita. He looked up, suddenly realized it was light, an ugly gray morning, but bright enough to see the redness in the men's eyes. The ambulance was gone, but the ugly blue and white trailer was still sitting there, smoking. He stared, not seeing, thinking he would go shower at the station, then drive his truck to Molly's house. He could see himself step up on her porch. She would still be sleeping. But it was morning, and he would wake her. He could see himself reach with his fist and knock loudly on her door.

First Flight

Lenore looked out at the farmland and drove. Brown cows stared out in the light. They put their heads down to the ground, yanked up grass with wide flat teeth and chewed. Lenore held the bottom of the steering wheel loosely in her hands, listened to the noise of the highway and the car moving in the wind. Ruth was leaning back with her eyes closed, and Roy was sprawled out in the back seat looking through his fishing magazines.

Lenore glanced at him in her rear view mirror. He looked like himself now, a boy, with his face relaxed, eyes softer; he looked years younger than he did an hour ago in the prison's visiting room. Lenore adjusted the mirror and looked at herself. She looked tired just like her mother had said. The eyes were bright, but her face looked dull, yes, tired.

They had sat in a circle in the visiting room, waiting for Dakota, waiting for their mother, yes that was their mother who came through the metal door. They had sat in a circle. Lenore, Ruth, and Roy had sat with one folding chair empty, waiting for their mother, yes there she was. She came to them smiling, holding out her hands. "My babies," she said, and she held them, she held them all in her arms, said "I've missed my babies." And all Lenore could think was you should have thought about that, you should have thought about that before.

How did a mother, how did a mother who dressed them once in dresses, shiny shoes, who put their hair in braids, who taught Sunday School, who fried chicken, drove a school bus, who did all those mother things, how did a mother wind up selling drugs, getting busted, getting locked up three years in the state prison? How did a woman, somebody's wife one time, somebody's mother, her mother, end up with those other women, all locked up in jail?

Easy. It had been so easy. With Mack, their father, a regular man, a fireman, a man who flipped pancakes in the air, a man who built a playhouse once in the corner of the backyard, a man who cried when his dog got poisoned once, that dog who limped in circle after circle, that dog who whimpered, head down, eyes up, limped in a circle till it slid to the ground, twitched, went stiff while her daddy, Mack, that man who put her mother in jail, her father, her mother, it had been easy for that man to call the detective to put her mother in jail.

Mack was mad, so it was easy. He hated that woman who took his kids, his house, and lived in broad daylight with a black man, a woman who sold drugs. It had been easy to hate the woman who had the black man run him off with a baseball bat, it had been easy to lock up the woman he had loved once. Yes he had loved her, Lenore had seen it, she had seen him bring her chocolate, Dakota had loved chocolate, and Lenore had seen Mack hide chocolate in the glove compartment in his pickup, had seen him slip chocolate out of the pockets of his overalls; she had seen him give chocolate to the woman he loved, the woman he also slammed against the wall sometimes, the woman he had kicked on the floor and beat with a chair once while Lenore, Ruth, and Roy had stood back screaming. It had been easy to lock her up. She broke the rules, so he did it.

Dakota was coming home soon. That was the last visit, that was the last time she'd sit in that room, watch Roy stare at the soda can in his hand, watch Ruth sit on the edge of her seat and chain smoke like a barroom whore. That was the last time she'd sit there, see the little black girl in the pink ruffle dress crawl in her momma's lap, eat M&M's from her hand like a little brown bird, that was the last time she'd sit trying not to see those matrons in their black skirts, black shoes, black hats, black eyes glistening, those shiny shields in the bright light, that was the last time her eyes would ache in that white light while she listened to her mother, that woman in jail, say "I'll see my babies home soon" while they sat in those brown metal chairs, eyes burning from the smoke, the light, the glistening metal while they waited, while they squeezed months of living into one hour in that room, while they waited for the bell to ring to say go now, enough visiting, go now, get up, get out, go home.

And they were going home now, driving through farmland now, for the last time without Dakota. Next time Dakota would be there, sitting in the passenger seat where Ruth sat now. Dakota would sit there, looking at the view like it was just another Sunday drive, while Lenore kept the car moving down the road, yes Lenore would be the one to bring her mother home. She would sleep on Lenore's couch, live in Lenore's house, a good house, a simple house, a neat house where everything stayed where you put it. But Dakota would be coming soon, and Lenore could see it already. When Dakota came, things would start to move. Glasses would break, pictures would shift crooked on the walls, pencils would roll off tables, slip under something, disappear across the floor. Nothing stayed with Dakota who could stir up a breeze just by walking in a still room. Yes, that was the last visit. Next time Dakota would be there, looking at the view.

Lenore looked at Ruth with her blond hair cut short, red heart-shaped earrings gleaming. Ruth had perfect red nails that tapped when she touched things. Now they tapped against the vinyl seat as if her hands were still at work hovering clicking over a calculator. Ruth liked numbers. They clicked. Ruth like clicking things, calculators, typewriters, fingernails. Her toes always tapped, fingers drummed. Lenore looked at Ruth sitting straight, staring out the window now, her fingers tapping as if she sat braced, ready, waiting.

She looked back at Roy's face and could see that he was deep under water with those fish. Dakota had taught him to fish. She had taught them all to love the sound of a lure splashing in water, the soft click of a reel, the tug of something hidden pulling a thin clear line. She had taught them all how to look at the flat gray surface of water and to see in their minds the movement of fish, the brown rocks quivering as the water moved. And now the water held him. She could see it hold as he watched the bright lures that whirred red and gold in dull water. Her baby brother was in the mind of a fish. "Good," she thought. "Good."

Lenore looked up at her mirror, saw the same dark green eyes like leaves. As long as she looked at herself, she wouldn't cry. She adjusted the mirror, straightened in her seat, and stared at the road.

She had always looked old for her age. Her mother's hippie friends used to pat her head and call her an old soul. "You might be fifteen, but you are an old soul," they said, and they nodded their heads as if they knew.

Even when she was a little girl, people called her granny because of her set ways of doing things, her way of telling Ruth and Roy to drink milk, clean fingernails, her way of telling them how to wear the right clothes. She watched them. Made order. Yelled when they wouldn't follow her plan. They called her granny. They were right, she had always been old.

They were riding through farmland. Just land and cows and corn. No woods for miles. Dakota Woods. With a name like that how could a woman be average? Named that because her mother had loved something about South Dakota where snow clamped down for months like a lid. The woman named her daughter Dakota as if the name could give a life wide flat plains and scattered seeds of gold.

Lenore passed a man with his thumb raised. He waved and lifted his head as if to say, "Slow down! Remember me!"

Lenore pressed the gas and stared ahead. All those drifters looked familiar. They moved across the land like spores carried in a breeze, touching everything, spreading like a fungus, sucking up life wherever they could land, spreading, leaving a sign of themselves, like disease. Lenore didn't have to look to see him.

She had seen him in all the others like him who once came to her house when Dakota opened the door, and opened, and opened and said, "Yes, my house is your house, come in."

And they all came in hungry, and they slept on the floors. And they patted Lenore's head and said, "Do you know how lucky you are to have a momma like that?" A woman who didn't believe in doors, who hated walls. Who opened the door and let the world rush in.

Dakota had run her house like a rescue mission. "They need me," she had said, when Lenore complained that she didn't have a mother, didn't have a room, a home. "Don't be selfish," Dakota had said. "Don't be so god-damned selfish. You've got to learn to give." And Dakota gave and gave and said "Yes, come in, what's mine is yours." And they took it. They took, and they slept on the floors, crawled into beds, under blankets, and washed their shirts in the sink and crouched in front of heaters and hummed and sank back in their own sweet smoke.

So Lenore didn't have to look to see the man on the side of the road with his thumb up, hoping for a ride. She knew his hair was scraggly, that dull shade of brown, and his teeth were yellow, wide and strong like horse teeth. They always smiled as if of course you knew them, as if you would know them, as if they knew you.

Lenore pressed the gas and leaned into the steering wheel. She knew drifters, knew a junkie at a glance. She had seen the hippies with peace signs, the bikers in leather who shot whiskey in their veins for lack of another drug. She had seen the skin mottled black and blue from burned veins. She knew the long-haired drifters who laughed like old men with wrinkled skin, ragged nails, who scratched the top of her head and said "Peace, baby," like it was a dirty word.

Lenore was fourteen when they first came like foreigners, in their scarves and beaded belts and headbands and denim and worn-out shoes. They sucked long pipes and short yellow joints rolled tight with spit, and they stared up at the ceiling through the thick clouds that filled the room. They spoke of Karma, Free Love, and Mother Earth.

Lenore had wanted the earth for a mother. She would walk in the woods away from her crowded house, and she would lie in the leaves, hold the earth with her arms, and listen to the ground breathe.

Her own mother was someone else then. Dakota had worn her hair in long braids, and she wore an African dashiki, its bright wide pattern hiding the body growing fat on whiskey and too much meat and potatoes.

When Lenore thought of those years, she couldn't remember where anything came from. Where did the clothes come from? The food? She couldn't remember shopping. It seemed that things just appeared like the people who came in the door. And Lenore couldn't remember their names, just the faces, the arm with the tattoo of a parrot, the sound of bells tinkling on a woman's belt. Lots of them wore bells, little brass bells that jangled when they moved. They all wore signs that meant something. Bells, flowers, doves, peace. They all worked so hard painting their signs of something. But what? Lenore could never learn the secrets behind the words, karma, peace, revolution.

She had asked, "What does revolution mean?"

"Freedom," they said.

"What kind of freedom?"

"Free love," they said, and they patted her head.

But she wondered, "Wasn't love free? Wasn't that one thing in the world that was free?"

Dakota had said love was free. She loved lots of men. She loved women too. Dakota could love anything that moved.

That year Dakota loved a black man. Jimmy who hardly talked, who couldn't look at Lenore who had thought even when he laughed, he looked ashamed.

"Black men are the most beautiful in the world," Dakota had said, and she would stroke his skin, touch his hair, say "Feel it, Lenore. Feel how soft." And Lenore would back away. She didn't want to touch anyone's head. She stepped back and watched her mother open the door, give free food, blankets, pillows, floors.

She could never understand why Dakota had married Mack. Why a plain Georgia-boy white man when Dakota had always loved dark men, black men? So why did she marry a plain old Georgia boy who smoked cigars, drank beer, and hauled scrap in the back of a pickup truck?

And why did the Georgia boy beat his wife until the black man ran him off with a baseball bat? Why did the Georgia boy leave his children with the woman in the dashiki, and with the black man and the drifters who blew in and filled the house like leaves?

Lenore was fifteen and skinny with big eyes and long hair when the men started touching her. They called her little sprite and patted her and said, "You might look like a girl, but you've got an old soul."

She had wondered, "What does that mean?"

And when the men tried to crawl into her top bunk at night, and her momma was far away laughing in the kitchen, and Lenore made her body stiff and kicked and thrashed until they gave up and slipped out, Lenore had wondered, "But what does that mean?"

Lenore was glad Ruth and Roy slept together on the other top bunk while the beds underneath were full of the drifters, the bearded men and bell-ringing women. Someone would always try to slip in her bed, but she sprawled out, rigid, not giving any room. "Don't be so selfish," her momma had said. But she wouldn't let them in. She would throw her arms as if fighting in her sleep. She drew her knees up, kept her eyes shut tight. And in time they crawled out of bed saying, "God damn, I'd rather sleep on the floor." And she could hear the others in the lower beds, hear them whispering as skin slapped skin and they all sighed and groaned and the drifters moved in the dark room full of bodies grinding, shaking the beds against the wall.

It was Dakota who had sent Frank in there, told him to go find himself a bed. Lenore had gone to her room to get out of the crowded kitchen, the house full of music, smoke, people laughing, sitting on the floor, rocking to a beat as they watched red candles. Lenore had tried to sleep, but she was awake when she heard Dakota's voice down the hall. "Go find a bed, Frank." And when he had found her crouched under her blanket, he whispered, "Oh, yes." And he pushed against her shoulders, said, "Oh, baby yes. You'll keep me warm." Lenore went rigid when she heard her mother's laughter in the kitchen. Didn't she know? Dakota was chopping carrots, making soup. She didn't know. The bells were tinkling and the music was playing and Dakota was thinking of other things. Lenore felt the thin hard body, the hairy hands that always touched her when he got near. He always touched the back of her neck, slid his finger up her arm. "Ticklish?"

Lenore turned face down and made her body stiff. He climbed on top of her. "I'll make you move." She held her body still while he moved over her, slid his hand under her tee shirt, down her hips. "I'll make you move."

Someone laughed across the room. "You be good to that girl."

Frank laughed. "Oh yes, I'll be good." He brushed his lips on the side of her face, ran his tongue along the back of her ear. "You ain't sleeping."

Lenore could hear the couple in the lower bunk. It was the big guy with a beard and the new girl from Ohio, the one who kept saying she was at Kent State as if it meant something. The girl had said, "I was at Kent State. I saw the whole thing with my own eyes." And Lenore had wondered what did she see. She wondered what the woman saw now, why the woman was letting the big guy with the beard grunt like a hog rooting in mud. Lenore listened to the man breathe in quick hard gasps. The girl was silent and the bed shook and Frank laughed. He held her face to him and ran his tongue along her lips, pressed it against her teeth.

She held her body stiff, and his hand moved over her legs. She thought, "I am a table. He is sanding me down." His hand pushed between her thighs. She held her body stiff.

Finally he quit. "God damn," he said. "Just go to sleep. I won't mess with you."

And she sighed, let her muscles go, let her breath ease. His hand pushed again. She clenched, and he laughed. The bed was shaking, and the man was saying, "Go, baby go." And Frank's hands were running over her, sanding her down. The couple in the bed below was laughing. The woman was saying, "Like that. Like that."

"That's love, baby," Frank said. He climbed on top of her, pushed her shirt up to her neck, yanked her panties down. He licked her. "Don't that feel good." And the bed was shaking and the room was pulsing with the sounds of mouths lapping, skin slapping as he licked her and worked his hands down while she pressed her legs tight and the whole room was shaking with the sound of mouths lapping, skin slapping. Lenore hoped Ruth and Roy were asleep. They were babies. What did it all mean, this love?

She heard Dakota laughing somewhere. They were all doing it. Free love. He was pressing on her. Dakota had said, "Move over, Lenore. Don't be so damned selfish." And the bed was knocking, and the room was grunting like it was all alive.

"It's like flying, baby," he said. They were laughing. Lenore wanted to fly. She wanted to be a cold metal plane slicing the air like a knife. He pushed, and she thought of the book she was reading about the Wright brothers, the boys who could fly, the boys who leaped from the dunes, made cold metal fly. Lenore made her mind think of the Wright brothers. They were in their bike shop, before they started work on planes. They were bending over a bicycle turned upside down. She could see them, two boys over a bike turned upside down, its gears exposed. They were spinning the pedals, watching the black chain jump. They were trying to find a way to make the machine light. They wanted the machine to fly along the ground. She wanted to fly. Their bodies were bent, and they worked on the machine.

He was cracking her open, "Come on," he said. She saw the black chain spinning around and around. She heard the whirring of the machine. She was the machine, and the wind carried her down a long black road. He drove into her while her head filled with the clanking metal noise. She saw the boys bent over the gears with their tools. They would tighten the machine.

"Move, baby," he said.

She was cold metal clanking while he cranked the pedal up and down.

Ruth touched her arm. Lenore was breathing hard shallow sounds, her foot pressed down to the floor, hands tight on the wheel.

"Are you all right?" Ruth said.

Lenore wiped her face with the back of her hand. "That place always depresses me."

Roy sat up and leaned forward. "Let's get something to eat," he said. "There's a Stuckey's. Pull in, and I'll buy you a milkshake." Lenore slowed the car and took the exit.

"Mom will be home soon," Ruth said. "It's almost over. We can have a real life. Like normal people. A life."

Lenore laughed. "A real life."

Roy touched her shoulder. "What kind of milkshake do you want? Chocolate, vanilla, pecan? Daddy gave me money. It's my treat."

Lenore smiled. "It's all living, huh? Mommas and daddies and milkshakes." She shifted into first at the stop sign. She sped across the highway and watched the traffic crest over the hill.

Across the Road

Stacey Lee sat in her front-porch swing and slapped the concrete porch with her bare feet. She pressed with her toes, pushed, and rocked back and forth. She listened to the creak of metal chain, wood, motion, and swinging she felt the slight breeze of an August morning on her freshly bathed and powdered skin.

Two teenaged boys drove by in a blue Ford and gave her a long look. Stacey Lee waved, thinking she might know them, or that they would notice the yard-sale sign nailed to the tree, and maybe they would stop in and buy. But they turned their eyes back to the road and drove on, so Stacey Lee grinned instead at her toenails freshly painted candy apple red to match her polka dot halter top, and she knew she looked pretty there with her blond hair damp and curly and her white cutoff jeans. She knew that from the road she didn't look thirty-nine and three times divorced. As she ate another cracker she told herself that she looked real good: her legs were tanned, her body still firm enough, and her eyes still big and bright blue. It was just her house that was showing signs of age. She looked down at the black ants scurrying for crumbs at her feet. She crushed a cracker in her palm, scattered it across the porch, and said "Eat, little devils. Eat me out of house and home, won't you."

What time and the weather hadn't rotted, the ants, termites, moths, and mice had eaten or carried away. At that very moment, the house, its boards, beams, curtains, clothes, food, and furniture were all disappearing, right in front of Stacey Lee's eyes, and she couldn't even see it, such small bites. All she could see was the sign of things going: the deep sag of the front porch, the window panes loose and rattling in their frames, the door knobs that fell out in her hands. Nails rusted, slipped from their holes, boards pulled from boards, paint bubbled and puckered so that a breeze, a rainstorm, or simply leaning against a wall could cause it to peel away.

Across the road she saw Hallie Rivers step out of her house and head toward her garden. Hallie Rivers was old. Her hands were brown and twisted like roots, and she hunched over as if she had spent her life carrying heavy loads instead of living like a lady on family money that came from buying and selling land fast after the Civil War.

Stacey Lee watched as the bent little woman hurried to her garden. She wore a wide-brimmed yellow straw hat and a bright blue print dress that flapped around her knees. She stooped, picked up things, and pitched them toward a pile of rubbish. Her arm was quick and strong. Stacey Lee whispered, "Old witch." She shook her head. "You might run this town, but you won't run me."

They had never spoken, but Hallie Rivers had once stood in the court house and called Stacey Lee "common white trash that should be swept out of town." She had tried to have Stacey Lee's house condemned, then tried to close her re-sale business down. And it was a good business, selling clothes, dishes, records, hubcaps, anything she might find when she went to yard sales in the late afternoon to buy up everything cheap.

Stacey Lee had a knack for junk. There was a trick to collecting, knowing what to keep, when to let go. It took luck. It took sense. More than anything, it took patience, and Stacey Lee didn't have nothing if she didn't have time. She could sit on things for years, just sit and wait because she knew that someday somebody could want anything, and she did her best to have it around.

She watched Hallie Rivers move down a straight and thriving row of plants. She stood and waved, but the woman, as always, stared down at her garden. Hallie Rivers moved down the row, hunched over, her arms crooked at her sides, her fingers stretched out, ready to snatch up the smallest weed. Stacey Lee couldn't see her face, just the hat bobbing, the bright dress flapping, and the arms jerking quick and mean.

Stacey Lee thought it was strange that a woman who seemed to hate living so much could be so good at growing things: a thick green wall of beans and peas climbed the trellis, fat red tomatoes bent their stalks, corn shimmered high and brightly reflected the sun in long curled leaves. She grew thick bushes of okra and vines of yellow squash, and radishes, lettuce, and carrots grew like something wild.

Stacey Lee shaded her eyes with her hand as an old black truck flashed down the road with its new paint shining, its chrome sparkling so brightly that she squinted and sucked in her breath. On the passenger's side, she saw an arm reach out and throw an empty can to the side of the road, and as the sound of the truck died away, she still heard the can roll and clatter into the ditch. Then she felt the quiet. Something about the way the black truck shined and moved so fast made Stacey Lee's head hurt right down to her teeth, and it wasn't the light or the way the engine whined as the driver popped the clutch and pressed the gas down hard, but something hurt. She moved to the shade on the side of the porch, and sitting with her back propped against the house, she pressed her closed eyes with her fingertips. She rubbed and watched the dark colors pulse and swirl.

When Stacey Lee saw old things looking bright and new, she was reminded of all the things she had let go. Not just cars, antique dishes, and furniture made of cherry and oak, but she remembered people, family, husbands, friends that seemed to pass through her life like good meals, enjoyed but gone.

As she leaned back and closed her eyes, she saw her dead baby, Marie, whose tiny dark face often appeared. Stacey Lee sometimes saw it in the grocery, or in her car at intersections, or taking a bath, eating breakfast, anywhere, just the face, dark, a little blue, big wet lips, ears almost pointed, and thick curly dark hair. She looked more like a cat, an elf, something else, not quite human. When Stacey Lee had seen her, born, dead, all in an instant, she wondered, "Where did this come from?" She had been born early, with an open spine, something Stacey Lee had never heard of, not her fault, just something that happened, misshapen from the start.

After Marie, Stacey Lee found the habit of letting things go. She left her apartment with its low ceilings and dark corners. She left her dog yapping at the door. She left her third and last husband drunk in a bar, and she left her baby buried far out in the country with no one but strangers and stone angels rotting in the wind.

When she heard Hallie Rivers' stories of how she had made a long rich life with no help from any man, with nothing but herself, when she heard the old woman's rule that a strong woman didn't need a man, and a woman needed nothing but a strong will and good sense, when Stacey Lee heard this talk, she wanted to slap the old woman with something dead. She knew that Hallie Rivers could never know of drunk husbands, black eyes, and babies born twisted and blue. A woman who had lived so pure, so safe, could never know the range of living.

Stacey Lee looked across the road. She hated that solid house that didn't rattle in the wind, and with a yard as rich as Eden. With the right breeze, she could smell the roses, the sweet purple wisteria, the musky camellia bushes that grew along the walkway leading up to Hallie Rivers' porch. Often, as Stacey Lee inhaled the scent of the garden, she felt as if it were a gift, and she was grateful, but sometimes, on a hot day, the sweet air was thick enough to choke on.

With the sun straight up overhead and the morning breeze gone, the day turned hot. As Stacey Lee stood and returned to sit in the swing, she saw the woman bent over, still working. She didn't stop, not to wipe her face, not for a drink of water, not for a minute's rest in the shade. Stacey Lee shook her head and whispered, "Even a dog's got sense enough to get out of the heat." At that moment the woman stood and stared so intently that Stacey

Lee looked down and kicked her feet, setting the swing in motion. When she glanced up, she saw Hallie touch her forehead with the back of her hand.

Stacey Lee looked at her own yard and tried to count the crates of tools, wire, glass, and pipes scattered and labeled for potential customers to see. An old wringer washer sat rusting by the road. A bookcase packed full of bottles, pans, dishes, and jars leaned against the oak tree. A pile of hubcaps glittered in the sun, and two rows of flower pots weighed down with rocks and dirt marked the path to the porch. On a post by the cinder block steps was a wooden sign that said in orange paint, "There's more inside!"

And there was. Almost everything in Stacey Lee's house was marked for sale. Stacey Lee had to make a living, and she had always believed there were more important things than things. But still, when she looked at her yard, and it seemed that the earth on her side of the road could grow only rocks and gray dirt, nothing like the rich black soil she saw plowed across the road every spring—when she saw the difference, she wanted more.

When Stacey Lee looked back across the road, Hallie Rivers was standing straight and staring. Stacey Lee stared back, but the woman kept looking as if she wanted her to do something. Stacey Lee stood up and yelled, "You got something to say to me?" Hallie stood there, her bright dress drooping around white stick-like legs. Slowly she raised her arms from her sides and held them out in front of her, reaching, holding nothing but air.

She dropped straight down to the ground. She fell so fast, disappeared so neatly behind a row of beans, that for a second, Stacey Lee thought it was a trick. Stacey Lee jumped off the porch, ran across the yard, and called from her side of the road, "Hey, you still there? You all right?" There was no answer. Stacey Lee looked and listened for some movement, but there was nothing. "Damn," she whispered. "Why'd you do this to me?" She looked down the road to other houses, but it seemed the world was asleep. No children playing, no cars, not even a dog, cat, or bird in sight.

Stacey Lee ran across the hot tarred road, her breath short and hard, feeling as if she were in a movie with the frames slowed down, clicking one at a time. She felt the grass under her feet. She could see the blue dress crumpled in the plants, white legs twisted in the dirt, thin arms splayed out, and the yellow straw hat leaning against the green beans. Hallie's face looked as gray as the dirt in Stacey Lee's yard. Her eyes were fixed, open, and seemed to stare up at the sun in defiance. Stacey Lee crouched next to her and carefully placed her arms at her sides and tried to straighten her dress. The woman's body moved as easily as a sleeping child. Her skin felt so papery thin and dry that Stacey Lee thought it might tear. She whispered, "She is dead. I am not screaming. This is how it is."

Stacey Lee lifted Hallie's head, and her pale dry tongue stuck out just barely, as if tasting for a drink. She tried to lick her lips and made a dry clicking sound. Stacey Lee had never seen a mouth so dry, the lips gray and cracked, the tongue looked plastic. She thought, "Water! Water, you idiot! Get her some water!" She ran across the garden, kicking up tomato plants, knocking down stakes. She ran shaking her hands as if she had just touched something hot. She found the water spigot and a jar on the porch. As she was running for the water, she looked toward the garden where the woman lay, and in her mind she saw Hallie rise up and chase Stacey Lee back home.

When she went back to the garden, she found Hallie just as she had left her. She touched her lips with the water, and Hallie's mouth sucked like something wild. Stacey Lee poured water into her palm and patted Hallie's face, neck, and hands, and she watched, waiting for the eyes to focus and see. Then Hallie blinked, tossed her head, looked at Stacey Lee with dark eyes and said, "You!"

"I saw you fall. Nobody else was around."

"You!" Hallie said again.

Stacey Lee nodded and helped her sit up. "You all right?"

"I'm breathing." Hallie reached for her hat. She stretched her arm out, then bent forward and covered her face with her hands.

"You ain't all right yet," Stacey Lee said.

"You don't know me. Shut your mouth." Hallie looked up. "What are you doing in my garden?"

"I told you. I saw you fall."

Hallie sat with her legs stretched out, brown lace-up shoes pointed straight at the sky and her dress twisted just above her knees. She sat and looked at her garden.

"I've got to get home now," Stacey Lee said.

Hallie shook her head. "Look at you. Bare-legged. No shoes. Feet filthy."

Stacey Lee stood and crossed her arms. "Didn't have time to dress. I thought you were dead."

Hallie's eyes wandered. "What's wrong with me, falling down like any fool in the sun too long."

Stacey Lee smiled. "An old pro like you ought to know better."

Hallie glared at her, then raised her hand. "Here, help me up." Stacey Lee reached down. Gently she held the woman under the arms and lifted. Standing together they looked down at the green plants broken in the dirt.

"Looks like you killed a few," Stacey Lee said.

"They're not dead yet." Hallie squinted down. "A couple of stakes. Some thread. They'll come back and grow." She bent toward the plants and started trembling. Stacey Lee reached and steadied her, and for a moment they stood holding each other, swaying a little, finding balance.

"Guess I'd better get you inside," Stacey Lee said, and she led the way toward the house.

In the kitchen she helped Hallie to a chair. "There," they said together, and they frowned into each other's eyes. Stacey Lee stepped back and watched Hallie, who glanced around the kitchen as if it belonged to someone else. The room was cool, and the windows were filled with leaves of hanging plants. Tall pine cabinets glistened, and the white tile floor shone. The round oak table at the center of the room was bare, and the counters were clear of cannisters, utensils, and things most people kept ready for use. Stacey Lee imagined for a moment that it was a fake kitchen, but there was a smell that made the room seem real. The air was slightly tainted with something that smelled like dirt, or plants sprouting, or skin, or blood. Stacey Lee stepped back and leaned against the door. "You look all right now," she said.

Hallie nodded. "A glass of water." She pointed. "In the cabinet there. You'll find them."

Stacey Lee nodded and turned on the water to let it run cold. When she opened the cabinet and saw the water glasses arranged in a neat row, then short clear tumblers, juice glasses, she knew that everything had been in the same place for years. There had been no one to misplace anything. She thought a blind person could live easily in such a house.

Hallie drank the water in long gulps. Then she set the glass on the table in front of her and held it between her hands. She glanced up at Stacey Lee, nodded, then looked down over the floor as if she had dropped something. Stacey Lee watched as Hallie's eyes searched the floor. She saw something and shook her head. "I knew it! She did it again."

"What?" Stacey Lee said.

"There!" Hallie pointed. "That crazy cat killed another one."

Stacey Lee saw a piece of something. "A mouse?"

Hallie shook her head. "That would make sense. Look!"

She saw it clearly now. The tiny furred head, eyes gouged out, skin peeled back on white bone, veins dangling like colored wires where a neck might be. "A kitten!" she yelled as she backed up to the counter.

Hallie shook her head. "She had four kittens. She's killing them one by one."

"That's crazy."

"It happens," Hallie said. "How was I to know the cat was female? It just came. Sniffing around my compost. It ate whatever it could find. Got fat. How was I to guess pregnant? Looked fat to me. Little thief." Stacey Lee listened, looking at the door, hoping for a way out, trying to think of something that would get her out the door and on the way home, but Hallie kept talking. "The cat just hung around here, mewing, scratching, started running into walls, chewing everything in sight. I couldn't keep her out. She'd run in, run out, live around me like *I* was the thief. I tried to run her off. Hit her on the back with a pan once. Thought it would kill her. She took off with a scream and came right back, just as wild. She's crazy. You'll see."

"I got to get home," Stacey Lee said.

"Last week she got into that broom closet, and quiet as night, had four kittens. She eats them, you know." Stacey Lee stared. "It happens," Hallie said. Something goes wrong somewhere. Happens all the time." Hallie looked around the room. She shrugged and looked at her hands. "That's the third one she ate now. Just found the second one out in the yard. Threw it in the compost with everything else."

Stacey Lee heard a soft thump somewhere.

"That's her," Hallie said. She watched Stacey Lee. "Yes, I've seen some strange things. Look at that little skull there. Bone frail as onion skin."

"Shh!" Stacey Lee said. Something fell and broke in the next room. "You sure nobody's in there?"

"It's the cat. You'll see."

Stacey Lee moved to the swinging door. Suddenly the cat pushed the door open and leapt into the room. She circled Stacey Lee, then crouched in the corner and stared up with yellow eyes set in her broad gray head. Her ears flattened, her belly pressed against the floor, she pulled herself across the room with quick jerks. She stopped, then with a leap crashed into the stove and bounced back to the floor. She saw the tiny skull in the corner and pounced, swatted, and the head spun across the floor. Stacey Lee jumped in a chair and watched as the cat glanced around the room. Finally she nudged the door open with her paw, and was gone.

"See!" Hallie yelled.

"That cat is sick. Bad sick."

Hallie nodded. "Looks like rabies, but it's not. Drinks plenty of water. God knows she eats. She's just mean. Evil. Sometimes I swear it's the devil himself."

"It's just a cat," Stacey Lee said. "A sick cat." She stepped down from the chair.

Hallie looked up. "Will you catch it for me?"

"No!" Stacey Lee said. "I didn't want to come over here. I don't even like you. Why should I put myself out for the woman who tried to close my business down. You deserve that cat."

A tremor started at Hallie's lips then spread through her face, her shoulders, hands. Her body rocked as she leaned forward on the table and cried. "What am I going to do?"

Stacey Lee walked toward the back door. "Call the humane society, I guess."

"My whole house stinks!"

"I know," Stacey Lee said. "About time you got a whiff of something rank."

Hallie sat up. "I can smell something rank anytime the wind blows from across the road."

Stacey Lee shoved a chair under the table and leaned into Hallie's face. "The next time you decide to die in the heat, don't look my way, lady."

"I never asked you for help."

"I never meant to give none. I saw you fall and just came running. You're lucky I didn't have time to think."

"Get out of my house! Trash. Nothing but trash. You ought to be ashamed."

Stacey Lee gripped and shook the table. "I had a baby once. You ain't never had a baby. You ain't never had a man. Too mean to love. I've loved three men and one baby. What you got? A bunch of plants."

"All I see at your house is trash."

Stacey Lee reached out and shook Hallie's shoulders. "I had a life once. It left me. But I had something. I kept trying to love. But it all went dead before I could hold it. While you been spending your life growing things, I've been losing pieces of my life all over this state. I hope that devil cat starts chewing on you. Let you lose some fingers and toes. Let you feel what it's like to lose."

She could hear her voice screaming. When she looked down, she saw the woman shaking her head and saying softly, "Help. Help." Stacey Lee looked at the wrinkled face, the dark eyes, dull, resigned, while the head was shaking no. Stacey Lee loosened her grip.

"I didn't know you were so old," she said. Hallie looked down. "I mean, I knew you were old, but you look so tough. Like you could plow that garden with your bare hands if you wanted." Hallie looked at her hands and tried to straighten her fingers, but the hands shook, and she held them tightly together in her lap. Stacey Lee stroked her arm. "I guess even you know what dying means."

Hallie didn't look up. "What are you going to do about the cat?"

"We're gonna call somebody. We need somebody. This kind of thing is a danger."

Hallie nodded. "What about the kitten? There's one she didn't eat yet."

"Where?"

"In that broom closet. She's probably saving it for tomorrow. Only takes one each day."

"Stop," Stacey Lee said. She moved toward the closet and listened. "I don't hear anything."

Hallie pointed to the skull on the floor. "That was today's kill. There's one left, I know."

"We've got to get it to the vet or something."

Hallie shrugged. "Probably going to die anyway."

"We've got to get it." Stacey Lee peered into the dark closet.

Hallie sat up straight and watched. "Just feel around there at the bottom. You'll find it."

Stacey Lee crouched down next to the wall and looked in. She thought she heard something and pushed her head deeper into the darkness. She reached, pulled back. She knew she would find teeth, blood, fur. She squinted, then clenched her eyes shut. Fingers stretched, shaking, she leaned into the closet and waved her hand in the emptiness and slowly felt her way toward the floor. She could hear nothing, just darkness, silence. Then she saw the face, the old face, her baby's face. She opened her eyes wide in the dark, bit her lip, and touched her fingertips to the floor. She searched, barely moving, listening. Finally she felt its warmth, fur, slight movement. She turned and smiled over her shoulder at Hallie who leaned forward in her chair. Stacey Lee scooped up the furry weak thing in her hands, held it close and sighed. She stood and said, "It's alive."

Blue Sky

Jack sat at the kitchen table in harsh yellow light reflected off walls slowly browning in grease and dust. His head was thrown back, mouth half-open, face unshaven, sagging, bloated. His legs sprawled out in front of him, his arms hung at his sides. The stub of a burnt-out cigar dangled between two fingers grazing the floor as he breathed deeply and shifted his weight against the chair.

He heard his wife somewhere. He heard her say something about going out to get Krystal hamburgers. He hated the greasy things, and she fed them to his girl for supper.

He tried to remember morning. It had been wet out and heavy with warm fog, barely daylight. He had shaken his little girl awake and said, "Look out the window, Katie." He had held her up to the glass and said, "Look, see what Daddy brought you. See the horse? See my baby's horse?" And there it was in the gray mist, a little swaybacked, potbellied horse tied to the mimosa tree. He remembered how she squealed like a little pig and ran out the front door barefoot, her pink nightgown flapping, her feet flying across the yard. Dancing around the horse, she had laughed and clapped her hands.

Jack heard his stomach gurgle. It burned. He licked his lips, tasted blood, and knew they were cracked. He wanted something wet in his mouth—whiskey, beer, even water would do. He wondered, "Where's Vicki? Where is that woman anyway?" He heard her moving somewhere. Drawers opened. Doors creaked.

He had seen the way men slicked back their hair and scooted forward in their seats whenever Vicki walked in a room. His friends smacked their lips like she was nothing but a sweet sugar-cured Virginia ham, and although they went on and on about her sense of humor, Jack knew it was the Virginia ham they were after. Watching the men, her eyes would flash and her red hair would shimmer with that quick toss of her head.

Jack sucked his lip and remembered how his friends had wanted Vicki to go deer hunting. "She can hunt like a man," they said, and she made it worse bragging that she shot rabbits as a kid and knew how to gig frogs in the moonlight. She was known for gigging a frog quick with prongs in the neck. She could take the quiver, the little gush of blood, and she didn't even flinch.

Vicki could play cards, drink beer, and go for deer just like a man. And the men loved it. They grinned so wide that once Jack had to knock her down in the leaves to make them stop thinking about his wife and start thinking about the deer they were after. And the men had just looked at him as if his own dead meat would be worth more than any ten-point buck. So he grabbed his gun and yelled that he'd bring back a deer if it killed him.

Jack remembered how he had hurried through the trees, hoping for a kill, looking so hard through the leaves that he didn't see the ground drop out from under him. He didn't see nothing but leaves and dirt and trees spinning against the sky while he tried to catch his breath, tried to stop the rolling down until he felt the ground slam, felt his leg snap like a stick. Flat on his back, he had looked up at the trees. His stomach rocked and colors blurred, so he breathed in and out until he could feel his weight against the dirt and know the pain without vomiting or screaming like a kid. He looked down at his leg burning and so heavy he wondered how it had ever moved. It was bent wrong at the knee, and his foot was twisted up over a rock.

He had yelled "Shit!" and then he felt for his gun in the leaves. Clutching the rifle to his side, he tried to move, but he retched and fell back into the dirt to stare up at the blue sky hanging above the green leaves going silver in the breeze. It was a sky that belonged in a picture book and not above a man broken in the dirt. Jack picked up his rifle and fired three times into the trees. "Damn you!" he screamed. He brushed at the twigs and leaves that fell over him, and he stared up. The treetops swayed in the wind just as before, and the sky looked even bluer in the afternoon light. He knew they would come for him laughing, joking, feeling sorry for poor Jack who couldn't walk through the woods without falling down. They would haul him up, carry him back to camp, and he wouldn't flinch or scream. He wouldn't feel the tendons pull, the bone grind. He would stare up at the blank blue sky and hate so strongly that they'd be amazed at his lack of pain.

And yes, they were amazed while he sat with his leg in the goddamned cast, while the skin itched, the leg burned. He never said how he retched when the doctor pushed and pulled at him like he was a piece of wood that couldn't fit into a groove. He never said how the crutches made his arms ache, never said how he wanted to wring her neck whenever she went out the door, stepped back in, said, "I almost forgot. Do you need anything?"

He had said, "Hell no, I don't need a god-damned thing."

But now the leg still hurt in rainy weather; his gut still clinched when he remembered them carrying him out of the woods; his chest still yanked inside when he remembered Vicki saying, "Damn, Jack, you'll never get a buck rolling in the leaves." But that was last year, and this year they'd see. He'd bring home a deer if he had to sit in a tree all damned winter. His leg might still burn on bad days, but he could hunt. The deer were thick this year, and Jack had a feeling this would be his season.

He heard movement somewhere in the house, and he tried to sit up because he knew if he slept she would rob him. She was always after money. Jack heard the TV sing and Katie laugh on the other side of the door. He wanted to hold her, wanted to see

those dark eyes all bright and happy. Yes, she was happy sometimes, and he wanted to see her mouth smile as she rocked back
laughing at some little thing on TV. Yes, Katie could be happy
sometimes. He could see her giggling, running with her skinny
legs so fast you'd think she was made of twigs and leaves, not flesh
and blood like him. Whenever he looked at his own fat belly,
his hairy hands, he couldn't believe that he helped make a thing
like Katie. Sometimes he thought a breeze just blew her in like
a dandelion weed, carried and dropped her into the dirt of his
front yard.

Jack wanted to hold her in his arms and feel her squirm laughing. He put his hands on the table, pushed himself up, and stood
there until he felt his feet solid and steady on the floor. With a jab
of his hand he swung the kitchen door open, and fighting dizziness
he moved into the living room slowly as if wading through mud.
Katie sat on the couch, holding a paper sack in one hand and
clutching french fries in the other. He could smell the warm
grease and salt. She looked up at him, pulled her feet under her
legs, and looked toward her mother.

"You bitch," he said. Vicki stared up at him. "Why don't you
get in there and cook? You make my girl eat this shit."

"I like Krystals," Katie said.

Vicki shook the ice in her drink. She sipped, then said, "Kind
of hard to cook with a drunk passed out on the kitchen floor."

Jack leaned, grabbed a paper sack off the coffee table and
crushed it, feeling the meat, bread, and grease still warm as he
mashed it into a ball and threw it at her face. Vicki flinched and
took a drink. Katie squeezed her french fries and stared at the TV.

"You like your horse, baby?"

"Yes," Katie said. She didn't look up.

Vicki said, "How much did you lose this time?"

"Didn't lose nothing that belongs to you, so shut your mouth."
Jack pushed himself forward and dropped beside Katie on the
couch. He saw her move away, but he reached out and patted her
leg. "So you like your horse?"

"Yes," she said.

"She said she liked it," Vicki said. "Now leave her alone."

"You don't want that shit your momma feeds you." He jerked

the sack from her hands and threw it on the floor. Katie drew her knees up to her chest and moved deep into the corner of the couch. He tried to smile. "Want to go get Kentucky Fried Chicken, honey?"

"No," she said.

Vicki reached for Katie. "Come here, honey. Sit on Momma's lap and finish your supper."

Jack jumped up before she could put a hand on Katie. He grabbed Vicki, yanked her to her feet. "Get in there and cook!"

"You don't want me to cook," she yelled. "You just want to hit me."

He grabbed her hair, pulled her head back, and slapped her. He saw her lip bleed.

"Go next door, Katie," she yelled, but Katie didn't move.

"Shut your mouth," he said. He stood over her with his fist pulled back, waiting.

"Jack, please," she said.

He hit, and she screamed, "Katie, run!" He slammed her head on the table. "Call the police! Run!" He slammed her head against the table again and again until she stopped screaming and slid to the floor. He looked up. The front door was open, and Katie was gone. The TV sang, and a blonde crawled half-naked on a bed. Jack watched. Then he yanked the plug and slammed the door.

He turned and saw Vicki on the floor stretched out on her side, hip curved and legs sprawled out. He dropped to all fours and leaned over her. He could smell whiskey on her breath. He lifted an arm and dropped it to the floor. He heard her breath. He lifted her hips and struggled with her pants, but she was too heavy. He fell down on top of her and moved, but his stomach rolled until he felt the sickness at his throat. He slid off her slowly and breathed to steady the room. "Whoa now," he thought. "Ain't never got sick on whiskey." But he was sweating and shaking like an old man, so he breathed slowly and put his face to the cool wood floor.

Sleeping, he dreamed that the ground went again, and he turned in colors until he slammed in the dark. Body burning, he stared up and cried until his throat ached and made no sound.

He was hungry, sick, cold, body swollen so hot and dry he felt it crisp like fat on a fire, and no one heard him call.

Jack pulled himself up and looked around the room. Vicki was still beside him breathing. He heard a muffled popping sound in the air. He looked toward the window and didn't know if it was getting light or dark. He heard movement in the kitchen, so he stood and headed toward the warm smell and bright light.

Katie kneeled on a chair next to the stove and shook Jiffy Pop over the red-hot burner. Jack watched the aluminum foil bubble, puff, and rise crookedly as if the steam inside were too weak, but the heat kept pushing, forcing it up through the foil. Katie stared at the pan and shook. Jack wanted a drink of water but knew he would have to stand near her to get to the sink. He sat in a chair and leaned against the wall. "Is it morning or night?" he said, trying to smile for her, but she just shook the pan and watched the foil rise.

"Almost night," she said without looking at him.

"I'm sorry, baby," he said.

Katie stopped shaking the pan. She reached to touch the foil dome stretched taut and smooth.

"Don't burn your hand," he said.

Katie picked up a fork and punched holes in the foil, letting the smell and steam puff into the air.

"You sure like popcorn," he said.

"Yes." She dropped a chunk of butter into a saucepan and put it on the burner.

"I love you, baby," he said. "You ought to have better than a sorry old drunk like me." Katie stared at the butter melting. "But your momma ain't no angel either."

Katie said, "I tried to call the police, but nobody was home next door."

Jack leaned forward. "You want you poor ol' daddy in jail?"

Katie didn't answer.

Jack said, "I brought you a horse."

"Momma says I can't keep it. She says horses can't be in city limits. Momma says you got a horse 'cause you were too drunk to win money." Looking at her, he could see Vicki's frown, the tight lips, and the two tiny wrinkles right between the eyes.

"You needed to pay the light bill," Katie said. He could hear Vicki's voice.

"The bitch," he said.

"I love my momma," Katie said, and she glared up at him with her bright eyes turned hard as glass.

"I guess you do," he said. He leaned over the table, grabbed the salt shaker, and slid it back and forth between his hands. He listened to the sound of glass sliding on the table top and the soft smacks as the shaker hit his hands. Katie stepped down from her chair to get a bowl. "So you don't like your horse now," he said.

Katie poured her popcorn into a bowl and reached for the hot butter. "Momma says he's so old and sick he'll probably be dead before I can take him for a ride."

Jack yelled and threw the shaker across the room, saw it hit Katie, saw the pan jerk, saw the butter splash down her legs. He jumped up, reached, and she swung the pan toward his face. He knew the butter couldn't be that hot, but she screamed.

"Oh, baby, I'm sorry," he said.

"It's all your fault!" She crouched behind the chair and gripped the handle of the pan. He had seen Vicki hiding like this, yelling that he was the one who made everything wrong. "It's all your fault," Katie said. "You burn my leg, hit my momma, and bring me a horse that's gonna be dead before I can take it for a ride."

Jack looked around for something to grab, something to break with his hands. He picked up a butcher knife and went to the door. "Bitch," he said, "I'll show you dead."

In the living room he saw Vicki sit up on the floor and wipe her mouth. He could have reached down and killed her quick, but he ran past her and out the front door. In the heavy mist he saw the horse still standing against the tree. Its head drooped to the ground, and its tail was tangled with leaves and mud as it stood there stupid, staring in the dark.

Jack circled and swung his knife. Katie cried, and he could see her moving somewhere. He jabbed, missed, and the horse tried to rear. He saw Katie untying the rope. He yelled, "Get back!" but she didn't hear. He swung the knife again. The horse reared up and punched with his forelegs like a man. Jack saw Katie fall, and he wanted to reach her, to get her safe. "Katie," he yelled, and then his head exploded, went red, then black. "Damn horse killed me," he thought as he slid into a wet dark. His skin tingled, and he rolled on his back and stared into the colors swirling, bright jagged lines, bursts of yellow lights. He felt the soft rain run sweet into his mouth.

He looked up at the gray mist hanging over his face. He saw the green mimosa leaves wave like fans, and he smelled the thick sweetness of the pink blossoms in the rain. He wondered if the horse would come back to kill him, but as he listened he knew the horse was gone, and Katie was gone too. All he heard was the sound of mist soaking into the leaves. And he felt the old pain, the sickness, the laying on his back and staring up at the trees and sky that looked down as if he were just another rock or clump of dirt. With his eyes closed he could see the blue sky floating over him, and he thought it wasn't gravity that kept a man from flying off into space. It was that blank sky that pressed everything down and held the world tight. Jack opened his eyes, watched the gray clouds grow darker, and he felt the rain push him deeper into the earth.

Power Lines

Thaddeus stood at the window and watched Hank ride the rake through the leaves. The boy's small high voice made something in Thaddeus shiver. He could feel the boy's heart pound, see the blood rush, hear the whoosh of leaves as the rake dragged along the ground. The blond boy with the face like an elf galloped around and around with his jacket flapping open, his feet pounding, his eyes squinting in the sun. "It's the boy," whispered Thaddeus. "It isn't me."

Thaddeus never made a sound, and even if he could move things in the living world, why would he? Why would a man dead for over a hundred years suddenly feel compelled to rattle silver, tip chairs, make clocks leap across the room. He leaned to the glass and said, "They always blame it on a ghost."

Thaddeus didn't think of himself as a ghost. The word never crossed his mind, except when a living voice said it. He had been a soldier in the Civil War, an orderly, because the Yankees wouldn't let the black men fight. The Southern boys always found the extra inch of strength if they faced a black man, so the black man stayed in the rear, digging latrines, tending horses. Thaddeus had died in the war, but he was not an angry ghost. He was simply in love.

He turned and saw the girl, Sarah, asleep, laughing in a dream. Her thick dark curls tumbled across the pillow, and her lips smiled as she brushed her hand over the stray curl tickling her cheek. He would have smoothed back the curls if he could. "You are lucky," Thaddeus said. "You are lucky Hank was born first. He saw a place in the world you didn't, so now he is screaming at the sky and you are giggling in a dream."

Thaddeus heard the door slam and Hank's boots thump across the floor. He slipped into the kitchen. Lavette, the boy's mother, was putting a chocolate cake in the oven. She stood and tucked the broken eggshells into a box and dropped it in the trash. She turned to the boy. "What do you need?" she said.

He wiped his nose with the back of his hand. "Water."

She handed him a napkin and went to the sink. As she filled the glass, Hank stood beside her and watched the water flow. Across the room, the trash can tumbled and the eggshells scattered over the floor. She looked at Hank.

He shrugged. "That's the ghost," he said. He gulped the water down.

"We don't believe in ghosts," she said. She bent and cleaned up the trash. "Your Aunt Jean put those ideas in your head. There's no such thing as ghosts."

He stared up at her. "So what made the trash jump out of the can?"

"I've told you," she said. "It's probably those power lines stretched over the house. You're not supposed to build under power lines. Electricity makes things jump."

He nodded and stared at the trash.

She turned on the faucet to wash her hands. "I read about it in the paper. Scientists say that power lines make things jump." She looked at him. "It's what the scientists say." He reached for a dishcloth. She had just put it on the counter. She turned and saw it on the stove. She never put dishcloths on the stove. It was dangerous. But there it was. She thought she had put it on the counter. She grabbed the cloth off the stove. "Go on outside," she said. "Your Aunt Jean's coming, and she's bringing company. I want to have the kitchen clean."

"I'm hungry," he said.

She gave him an apple. "We'll eat cake later."

"I don't want an apple," he said. He put it down on the counter, turned and stomped across the room. Lavette watched the curtains shake as he closed the kitchen door. She leaned against the counter. The curtains still moved.

She wiped the counter and set out toothpicks for testing the cake, racks for cooling, and the ready-to-spread frosting in its aluminum can. She paused by the window and breathed as the warm smell of cake slowly filled the room.

It was her sister, Jean, who believed in ghosts. Thaddeus didn't like Jean. He didn't see how the two women could share the same blood. Lavette was smart, but Jean would believe anything if a magazine said it twice. "Once makes it chance," she always said, "but twice makes it fact." So now Jean was coming and bringing a witch who was supposed to run out the angry ghost. "It isn't me," said Thaddeus. He moved closer to Lavette to watch the words rush under her skin.

Lavette crossed her arms and looked at her kitchen. It was clean. Her boy was healthy and running in the leaves. It all looked fine. Her house was steady. It just shook sometimes. Lavette sighed and watched the clock. She could see Sarah sleeping. She hoped the witch would come and go, and her girl would sleep through the whole thing. She loved the smell of Sarah sleeping. She had a different scent then, heavy and sweet, as if a mist surrounded her, protected her dreams.

Thaddeus held Lavette's hand, but she thought she held only herself. Thaddeus loved her kitchen, warm and small and crowded with smells of food. He stood behind Lavette and saw the sweat glisten on her neck. Her cake was cooking, almost done, he knew by the way the scent filled the room, golden particles swirling up from the oven pressing softly against the walls as the cakes took form and turned deeper brown.

He felt Jean coming and shuddered. The door flew open and she stepped into the room.

"Where's the witch?" Lavette said.

Jean put down her purse and sat in a chair. "She wanted to drive herself. I drew her a map. She'll find it."

Lavette shook her head. "She can't be a real witch if she needs a map."

Jean glared up. "Her name is Betty Pryor. She's a genuine white witch. This isn't a joke." Thaddeus laughed and felt the air stir.

"I don't want a witch," Lavette said. "I just want my house to stand still.

Jean stood and pointed to the window. "Well, you asked for it. Nobody with good sense lives in a house on the edge of Chickamauga Battlefield. Thirty-four thousand men died in that field."

"People die all over," Lavette said.

"But it's sudden death that makes a ghost," Jean said. "Makes a man mad to die too quick. Ain't nothing like a war to make a bunch of mad ghosts. It's common sense."

Lavette turned and took the cakes from the oven. "I still don't believe in ghosts."

Jean stood and yelled, "You can't put a dishrag down in this house and be sure it will be there next time you turn around."

"Kids move things," Lavette said. "Keep your voice down. Sarah is asleep."

Jean tightened her lips, then whispered, "I was here when that bag of coffee jumped to the floor, and Sarah and Hank were sitting right there at that table eating ice cream. How do you explain that?"

Lavette tested the cakes. They were smooth and brown. She lightly pressed her hand over the warm surface. Thaddeus could feel the warmth enter her skin.

"There's a word for what's happening here," Jean said. Haven't you heard of a poltergeist? The spirits get angry and throw things. It happens all the time."

Lavette turned the cakes out to cool. "I've said yes, Jean. This woman can come and do what she wants." She looked at the clock. "Where is she? Her broom break down?"

Jean sat and opened her purse. "Remember, I'm paying for this. The least you could do is be polite."

Lavette sat with her. "I'm tired to death already. I don't want to mess with a ghost."

Jean stared at the walls. "Well you've got a ghost that wants to mess with you. There's evil in this house."

Lavette looked at her kitchen. She saw the hole in the wall where the phone used to be. She had meant to plaster over it, but she had hung a calendar there and the calendar kept falling down. She remembered her husband, Larry. She remembered when he pulled out the phone. She remembered dishes smashing on the floor, the crack of his fist on her skin. She looked at Jean. "If you ask me, I'd say any evil in the house comes from the living, not the dead."

Thaddeus stroked her hair, but she didn't feel it. He wanted to hold her. He wanted to hold her and Hank and Sarah. He wanted to touch them all.

Jean looked at the hole in the wall. "That man's been gone for years."

"He's the only ghost that worries me. And he's alive."

Thaddeus slipped from the room. There were marks of the man all through the house. Even in the children's room with the soft toys, the bright pictures, puzzles, and books and cars and dolls that made soft cooing sounds, even there, he saw signs of the man who had lived there. He saw the lamp, the ugly little pink lamp. Thaddeus heard the words scream. The lamp carried the voice, "I hate you, little bastard." Thaddeus saw the man throw the lamp at the boy's back, saw the light bulb shatter, fly into the fine blond hair, and the voice screamed, "I'll stick your finger in the socket, boy. Don't you say a word." Thaddeus heard it. "I'll plug your finger in the socket. You'll sizzle into smoke." Thaddeus saw Hank stare at the man, his daddy. He had stared and nodded, folded his arms, kept his lips firmly, tightly closed.

Thaddeus heard the boy scream, and he moved to the window. But the boy was yelling at the sky, while the voice from the lamp still screamed. He wanted to lift the lamp and throw it out, pitch it to the bottom of a well, where the water and earth could bury forever the awful noise.

Thaddeus stood at the window and watched Hank run. He felt the blood rush from heart to fingertips when the boy squeezed his plastic toy gun that shot a popping noise in the breeze. Thaddeus listened to the leaves go whoosh, smelling of earth, crackling like fire across the ground.

Thaddeus turned and watched Sarah reach for the red sweater she loved more than any toy. Long outgrown, stained, worn to threads at the seams, it belonged in the trash, Lavette said, but Sarah said no. She reached for it in her dreams, but it fell to the floor, so she hugged the blanket, rubbed it under her chin.

Thaddeus watched the sweater lying on the floor in the shadow under the bed. He wanted to reach, shake out the dust, and place it next to her cheek, where she only dreamed she held it. But there it sat in the dust, because Thaddeus couldn't move a thing in the world without the help of a human hand.

He bent to the sweater and saw the dust cling. The red yarn shimmered. Even as it sat there, a heap of red cloth in the dark, it moved. The living eyes couldn't see it, but air pulled at threads, dust settled, cloth gave its shape to the dark. "It's all moving," Thaddeus said. "Everything is moving by itself." Outside he heard the boy still running, his voice fading into the sky. Thaddeus went to the window and watched the boy's face twist with his cries of war. So much noise for one small boy. Thaddeus wondered, "Will the witch see?" If she is a real witch, she will hear the boy's screaming and know it isn't me."

Betty Pryor knocked softly three times on the front door. Thaddeus slipped through the walls to see the woman who claimed she could make spirits move. He had never seen a white witch, just the black one who came when he was a boy sick with fever. The black Hoodoo witch was squat and broad with arms like a man's and eyes like a fox, hard glancing eyes that watched for a misplaced hair, a lost fingernail, a drop of urine that could be a sign of a spell cast on someone in the room. She was an ugly witch, but the garlic and mustard pouch she tied around his chest pulled the fever out. The glass of horse piss she had placed by his bed drew the evil from the room. When she poured the piss under a hemlock tree deep in the woods, Thaddeus was cured.

He wanted to see the kind of magic a white witch could do. Lavette opened the door, and Thaddeus saw the silhouette of the small woman standing in the sunlight. She nodded and walked into the room. She was a tiny woman with wide gray eyes, thin lips, and hard little face. Thaddeus thought she looked like a sparrow. She wore a black dress that draped loosely except where it was gathered at the waist and held by a red sash. In her long white hands, she carried a plastic K-Mart bag. Thaddeus laughed and watched her move. Her legs were thin and stuck straight down to the floor where they ended in tiny feet pressed into black cloth shoes.

Thaddeus thought of sticks walking. He remembered the wooden toy his momma made for him once, a stick boy supported by strings between two strips of wood. When he squeezed the wood, the boy jumped and flipped in a regular, jerky motion with stick arms and legs flying out, around and around, the wood making tiny clicking sounds. He would squeeze again, and the stick boy would jerk and tumble into a new contortion on white strings.

Betty Pryor nodded and circled the room. Jean stared and waited for a sign. Thaddeus could hear Jean hoping that books would fly, a lamp shake, or a knife would jump across the room.

"Yes," the witch whispered. "Someone is here."

"Right," said Thaddeus.

Lavette stood in the kitchen door. "You'll have to keep it quiet. My baby girl is asleep."

"I am quiet," the woman said. "It's your spirit who makes the noise." She circled the room and studied the walls as if a spirit could leave a fingerprint for a living eye to see. "The world is like a cake," she said. "There are layers we can't see until we take a knife and slice deep to its center." She nodded her head. Thaddeus watched the gold hoops in her ears bang against her jaw. "There are things in this world we can't see," she said. Suddenly she stuck her hand flat into the air. "A world is moving right there."

"Really," Lavette said. "What do you see?"

"Frustrations. Pain." She stood in the center of the room with her eyes closed. "It is an angry spirit."

"It's the boy," said Thaddeus.

"A dangerous spirit." She opened her eyes. Thaddeus moved a little closer to see if she could feel the air move. But the woman kept hopping around the room like a hungry sparrow. She stopped, cocked her head, listened.

"You hear water in the pipes," Thaddeus said, "the electric hum of the refrigerator, the ticking clock, nothing but machinery, human noise."

"I hear something," she said.

"Greetings from hell," Thaddeus said loud enough to shake the house, but the woman didn't flinch. She was deaf as a stone.

Lavette stood at the kitchen door and wiped frosting from her hands. "You hear my water pipes," she said. "There's nothing here. Come sit down and eat some cake."

Jean followed the witch. She stopped and shook her finger at Lavette. "So what makes things fly across the room?"

"I told you. Electricity. Sometimes electricity makes things jump."

"This house has a spirit," the woman said. She peered down the hall leading to the children's room.

"It's the boy!" yelled Thaddeus.

"Maybe it's psychic energy," Lavette said. "I read about that. Sometimes our mind does things."

"Right," said Thaddeus. He wanted to kiss her for saying the truth.

The witch pointed to the children's room. "He is there," she said.

They moved down the hall to where Sarah smiled in her sleep.

"This is where your spirit hides," the woman said. Sarah turned, and her eyes flickered as she started to wake. The three women stood watching as if she were a moth slowly, silently shaking from her cocoon.

"He is here," Betty Pryor said. She lifted a crystal necklace over her head and hung it in the window. Purple and white fragments of light splattered across the room. She pulled sticks of incense from her shopping bag. She lighted them, then placed them in four corners of the room. Again, she reached in her bag, pulled out seven white candles and a gold cross the size of her hand. Sarah sneezed and sat straight up. She stared at the incense, the candles, the strange woman in the black dress at the center of the room. She sucked in her breath, reached for her mother, and began to cry.

Lavette lifted her up. "Let's go, baby. Momma just baked you a cake."

The witch reached in her bag. Thaddeus wondered what sort of magic she would try to do. She hung more crystals and bunches of herbs throughout the room. She laid a cross in every corner. Thaddeus thought her tools were very pretty, but they would never match the power of a goat's foot roasted and wrapped with leaves and twine. He knew pretty things would do nothing to soothe the spirit shaking the house.

The woman stared at Jean. "This is an evil room. Feel it?"

Jean nodded. Thaddeus saw Sarah laughing in the kitchen. He saw Hank was mashing crumbs of cake with his fork and swinging his legs in furious rhythm under the table. Lavette smiled at her children and poured glasses of milk while the two women stood determined in the children's room.

"Feel the cold?" the witch said. Jean nodded and rubbed her arms.

Lavette called from the kitchen, "Would you ladies like some cake?" Thaddeus heard the kitchen chair scrape and Lavette's footsteps as she came down the hall. She stood in the doorway. "You are crazy," she said.

"No," Jean said. "Feel him. Feel the cold?"

"He is there," the woman said. She pointed to the closet.

Thaddeus stood in front of Betty Pryor's face. He smiled and turned to look at the tiny closet where he knew there was nothing but shoes, shirts, dresses, hats, and a dead bug curled in the dust on the floor.

She moved toward the closet slowly. "I am here to help you," she said. "I want to help you move along to the other side." Thaddeus hovered behind her and waited for her to name what he knew wasn't there.

"He's a Confederate soldier," she said. "He is leaning on a homemade crutch, and he has an arm in a sling. He is young. Blond. He died in the woods outside. He says he's hiding from Yankee soldiers, and he wants to go home."

Thaddeus laughed and said, "Why do all your Southern ghosts have to be Confederate boys? They are always blond. Blue eyes. Sweet wounded Southern boys."

The women stood with their skin prickling, their faces dull and white as dough.

"It's Hank," Thaddeus said, "Not your blond soldier. It's the boy who is screaming. Listen!" Thaddeus wanted to throw something, but he could only move to the window. "Yes, there are layers of life here, layers of pain."

The woman only saw her blond, blue-eyed boy. She spoke to

the closet. "Let go of this world. Turn toward the light. Your friends are there. Your mother. Go, and you will find peace."

Thaddeus wished the woman were right. He wished death were just a matter of turning toward the light. But it wasn't easy to turn from where the spirit could draw love from the world through fingers, eyes, ears, mouth and tongue. He wanted his body, but he didn't miss the pain. He was safe now from the whip, the rope, the knife, the gun, the force of a man's fist pressed deep against skin, nerve, muscle, bone. His body was safe now, pain was just a sound rising and falling back again to the hard ground of the living world. His body was safe now, and that was one good thing about being dead.

He looked out the window to where his body had died, where Sarah liked to dig in the dirt, and Hank shot at the trees. It was in the clearing, where once a stand of sycamores grew, it was there where he left his body on the ground. After a hundred years, he could still feel the hot iron ball sink into his chest. He remembered how the heat spread, the chest grew hotter. Hands, feet, legs went cold as the chest burned. Slowly the warmth slid from his limbs and sank toward his chest, like water whooshing, sucking, spinning down a drain. The life slid down toward his center and fell through the hot dark hole to the other side. His blood seeped out and warmed him, and he thought, "Yes, nothing holds me to this world."

He had said yes to the hot blood seeping out of his chest. He had said, "Yes, this is the warmest place I've ever been." Thaddeus remembered how once when he was a baby sick with the croup, his momma held him over boiling water to catch the steam, and he cried and breathed. Her hands were wide and strong as she held him. Then she rubbed him head to foot with a paste of lard and onions, and he cried, and her wide warm hands pushed and rubbed as if she could force the sickness out the way she squeezed the liquid out of a sack of homemade cheese.

As he lay there dying in the woods, he could feel her warm hands hold his back, press deep in his chest, and he coughed black blood and spit on the ground. His momma's hands held tighter, pressing the evil out, and then her hands held gentle, steady, and warm until he was slick as a wet seed. Her hands soothed, pressed all the life blood toward the center of his chest, until he could breathe a little easier, and let his arms fall to his sides, let his legs stretch out on the ground. He could breathe and sink into her warm hands.

He was dead when the white boys found him. They bashed in his head and cut off his testicles and threw them in the trees. He was already dead, so they couldn't touch him when they dragged his body over the ground. From high in the sycamore, he had looked down at the stupid Southern soldier boys. Not a single one was blond, and they weren't handsome, with their stinking flesh, matted hair, and rotten teeth. And he laughed because he knew they were dying too. It would take a little time, but they would feel the pain. Thaddeus was dead, and he knew.

Suddenly Betty Pryor stepped back and Thaddeus shivered when she passed through his space. "He is crying now," she said. "The boy will go now to the other side." She stood nodding at the closet. Tears ran down her face. Jean leaned against the wall and hugged her own arms. Thaddeus moved in front of Betty Pryor's face. If he were alive, his breath would make the woman's hair tremble. She waved to the closet. "Go on," she said. Her hand moved through Thaddeus. He shuddered and moved away.

"Good-bye," he said as they turned and left the room. The incense curled and rose in the pulsing candle light. Thaddeus watched the dust settle on the red sweater under the bed. It was slowly wearing down, collapsing into the gravity of the earth. Another thread pulled free, a thread so small only Thaddeus could see the slow unraveling.

He heard them talking in the kitchen, rattling silver, the clinking sound of the cake knife against the glass plate. He heard Lavette's silent words saying she wanted the day to be over. She wanted her sister and the woman to eat their cake and go. She wanted her children in the kitchen, swinging their feet under the table as they ate and laughed and talked of what they could be.

Thaddeus reached out and tried to hold the sweater. He wanted to hold it near his heart. He heard Betty Pryor call from the front door, "The spirit is gone now. You will live in peace." And finally she was gone.

He watched her little blue car vanish down the road. "No," he said. "The evil is here, and it isn't me." He would never leave the place where his living blood spread dark and warm into the earth and fed the creeping cypress dense and green along the ground. "That is me," he said. "I am there where the frogs belch deep croaking sounds, where the crickets chatter long and loud." They had all been fed by his blood, his only and final sign of life. So he would stay and listen to the birds, the trees, the leaves sigh as they tumbled down to the ground.

He heard a loud smack in the kitchen and Sarah scream. He moved through the wall and saw Hank standing at the door and staring down at his dirty sneakers as if they would run if he gave them a chance. His face was pale, and he bit his lip. He stood with his thin shoulders hunched, jaw tight, as if he were ready for a blow to the back of his head. Lavette held Sarah and screamed, "Why did you do that, Hank?"

Hank ran out the back door.

"Stop right there," she yelled. He stopped, turned, and stared at his mother through the screen. "Why did you slap your sister?" He shrugged and looked off at a crow flapping to a higher branch in a tree. "What made you do that?" Sarah was sobbing, gasping, and she leaned into her mother's chest as if she could find her breath there. Thaddeus saw Hank's red finger marks blossoming underneath her white skin.

Hank pointed his gun to the sky. "Electricity," he said.

"What?" Lavette yelled even though he stood just on the other side of the screen.

"Electricity." He pointed to the wires stretched over the house. "You say the power lines over the house make things jump. My hand jumped," he said. He stared at his mother with cold deep dark eyes. "It wasn't me," he said. He turned and ran out into the yard.

"Come back here," she yelled. She stepped out on the porch and stroked Sarah's hair. She glared at Hank who was already on the rake and staring at the ground as he pulled the metal prongs through the leaves.

"Come back here," she called. Thaddeus stood behind her, wanted to hold her and tell her to let the boy go because he was already gone. Thaddeus could feel the tightness in the boy's throat, saw his eyes squinting in the sun. The boy tightened his grip on the rake. He would not cry. Thaddeus wanted to glide out and hold him. He sighed to the silent room, "It isn't the boy. It is the man, the man who shaped the boy with a fist." And Thaddeus knew the boy couldn't say why he hit his sister. The boy didn't know. To the boy, the hand jumped, just the way his father's hand jumped through the air and yanked him into pain.

Thaddeus looked out and saw the crows swoop and settle on new branches. Starlings fluttered and roosted on the power lines stretched like gray bars over the house. Sarah breathed quietly, and Thaddeus heard Lavette's heart pound. He heard the power lines hum and looked up to where the starlings were settled, stretched out in a neat row, silent, still, and watchful, as if they were standing guard.

"Hank, come here," Lavette said. "Please. Listen to me." But the boy didn't hear his mother call. He rode his rake around and around. The electricity hummed, and the leaves went whoosh as the rake scraped along the hard ground.

Noises

Connie remembered how for months after Trisha was born, she would wake in a panic suddenly in the night. She would swear she had heard something: a gasp, a cough, or even too much silence, but something screamed "Danger!" and Connie would bolt from her bed and run to her daughter's room. She would touch the baby's face, lift an arm, jostle a shoulder, do something that would make the baby stir and let her mother know that yes, of course, she was still alive and safe.

Looking at her grown daughter's face Connie remembered that old panic, but now there was a reason. At twenty-six, Trisha was filthy and so drunk that her words slurred and spit flew when she talked. Her bottom lip was cracked, caked with dried blood, and her eye was bruised, her cheek swollen, her nose smeared with blood and dirt. Connie reached for her.

"That's it!" Trisha said. "He's done it this time, by god." She leaned back on the couch and slowly exhaled smoke from her cigarette.

"I hope you mean it," Connie said, knowing the old line repeated, "I'm leaving," then the loneliness of leaving, the running back, the constant running back again.

"Of course I mean it," Trisha said. "I've had enough. I told him. I said, 'You hit me one more time, Jimbo Jones, and I'm leaving, I swear.' Then he hit me again! See?"

"I see it," Connie said. She reached for her daughter, pulled her close to her chest, smelled the oil in her hair, thought, "How did my little girl get so dirty?"

Trisha jerked away. "It hurts my neck when you do that." She started to cry. "I've been hurt enough already. Just leave me alone."

Connie sat back on the couch. "You don't have to live with him. You've got a home right here if you want."

Trisha shook her head. "Don't you have any cold beer or nothing?"

Connie got up and made Trisha a Coke. She wanted to kill this Jimbo Jones who used to love her daughter. He did love her until she got drunk, then he got drunk, and they started circling each other like two dogs finally released from their chains. Connie put the tall cool glass on the table in front of Trisha. "He'll kill you one day," she said.

Trisha stared at the floor, took a sharp breath. Connie watched her hand clench into a fist, saw the fist beat softly one, two, three into the cushion of the couch. "He won't kill me," she said. "He loves me. He's just crazy sometimes."

Connie went to the door to make sure it was locked. Nobody ever doubted that he loved Trisha. Anybody could see it in the way his face went soft and warm when he watched her do something as simple as scramble an egg. Connie remembered watching him watch Trisha make potato salad for the Fourth of July picnic. It was supposed to have been a good day, a day when they both promised not to drink, not to fight. They had promised. And it had started to be a good day, in Connie's kitchen with Connie frying chicken, Trisha making the salad, and Jimbo sitting at the table, drinking coffee, smiling, peaceful as a prince. "He's a prince," Trisha had said. "I finally got me a prince, Mom." And that day he did seem like a prince, so calm, so happy, so soft and warm when he watched Trisha move across the floor, looking so sweet Connie couldn't help saying, "You really love my girl, don't you, Jimbo."

He nodded once and looked at his coffee. Connie said, "He couldn't live without me, Momma. He told me. Couldn't get up in the morning if he didn't have me."

"Shit," he said. But he was grinning, that strange grin, the way Larry used to grin when he looked at a poker hand, knew he was losing, knew he couldn't let that loser's hand show. But Trisha was peeling potatoes and didn't see it. So Trisha said, "It's true, Jimbo, you said it. You couldn't live without me."

"Like hell." He looked at Connie. "She's good in the mornings, but you get her out drinking, she's nothing but a goddamned whore."

Trisha had stared at the potatoes. She wouldn't cry, but Connie could see that she could break any second from the way she held her mouth set tight and closed, while her hands moved like there was nothing else in the whole world but peeling potatoes.

Connie knew that game. It was an old game that Trisha's Daddy had played. Connie had called it the black turn game. She had seen it a hundred times before, and now she saw it in Jimbo: that soft look of a boy in love turn in a second to something mean. The man could be happy as a prince until you said the wrong word, made the wrong sound that could make a man in love swoop like a hawk ready to grab anything that dared to move across the ground.

Connie could hear the old words screaming, "You asked for it!" Larry had always said that just after the hit. Now Jimbo said the words. Now even Connie said the words when she was shaking Trisha by the shoulders, yelling, knowing that Jimbo wouldn't hit Trisha if she would just behave. "You asked for it!" Connie had said to her own daughter who stood there bleeding, saying, "Momma, he did it again."

Now she looked at Trisha, wondered, "Did anybody really ask for that?" She reached for her daughter's hand. "He's gonna come for you," Connie said. He would come crying, want to talk, make up, then he'd buy her flowers, a new sweater, buy something as a promise, the old promise: "If you be good, I'll be good," then they would start all over. That was the only promise. They would go round and around and around, mad dogs circling again.

Now Trisha was laughing, holding her hand to her mouth to sooth the torn lip. "Damn right he'll come for me," she said. "As soon as he finds I'm gone. He thinks I'm locked in the bathroom. Guess he forgot about windows." She smiled and tapped her head with her finger. "He might be good-looking, but he ain't too smart. I climbed out of that window like a ten-year-old boy. Good thing I'm tough. I'm too tough for him, right Momma?"

"Right," Connie said, thinking, "Wrong," feeling in her chest that old panic at the wrong sound in the night. Trisha would never say the right thing, and as long as Trisha said the wrong thing, took the wrong step, Larry would be there to swoop down and grab her and squeeze until she bled in his hands.

"Why don't you get some sleep," Connie said. "I got to clean the kitchen."

"I hurt too bad to sleep. Don't you have a cold beer?"

"No." Connie stood and turned off the lamp. Trisha sighed and lay down. From the door of the kitchen, Connie watched as Trisha groaned and shifted her body on the couch. "At least she's here," Connie thought. She stood and listened to Trisha's breath rise and fall. The living room was dark except for the new street light that shone through the curtains. All around the house stretched silence and darkness except for the one light that made Connie happy because it meant that the city was growing toward her house where there was nothing but woods, rabbits, birds, and a black-top road that was hardly used.

From where Connie stood, Trisha looked like a child who had fallen asleep in front of the TV. There was her baby girl, the girl who once left wild flowers in a vase at the front door and a card to Connie signed "Love, Elvis." Trisha who was once always trying to find a way to get her momma laughing. They both had loved Elvis, spent afternoons together in the front-porch swing, rocking, singing "Love Me Tender," the only song they both knew well enough to sing all the words. Connie took a blanket from the closet to cover Trisha, and as she leaned she smelled the stale cigarettes, sour whiskey, and a faint musky body odor that made her wonder when Trisha last had a bath. Trisha snored softly, and

Connie wanted to kill Jimbo Jones who once broke her daughter's nose.

She went to the kitchen, ran the water hot, and filled the sink to wash a few dishes. She thought she should mop the floor or clean the shelves. She wanted the smell of bleach, ammonia, lemon, pine. She wanted to be strong enough to throw Trisha in the shower and lock her in with the soap and steam until Trisha could stand straight, smell sweet, and smile.

Connie remembered how Trisha used to be so pretty with those brown eyes and dark skin like her daddy, her daddy's girl all right with those eyes flashing and the sad way of getting wild after just one beer, that one beer that could make most people happy, but made Trisha, like her daddy, throw her head to the side a little and say something loud and mean.

Yes, Connie believed it when Jimbo said Trisha would start on other men when they were out drinking. Yes, Connie believed Trisha would grin at other men, say Jimbo didn't make enough money, Jimbo snored at night, say Jimbo couldn't get it up, say anything to let Jimbo know he didn't own the words that could fly from her mouth. Sometimes even Connie thought Trisha deserved getting smacked. Who could blame him? But when she had seen Trisha's face, the lip torn, eye swelling, the purple, yellow welt spreading across her skin, she had thought, "Nobody asks for that."

Connie could hear the voice again, someone's voice, rushing, rumbling, cracking like a summer storm, "You asked for it!" Larry screaming, her own voice screaming "Larry, please," then Trisha, crying "Please, Jimbo, stop hitting me." Connie heard it, the sad wailing scream, "Please."

Jimbo could be polite. "He's a prince," Trisha had said. And even Connie thought he might be that day she first met him in the hospital room. They had thought she was dying then, and everybody was polite when they thought you were dying. Jimbo was sweet as a puppy that day Trisha brought him to the hospital, "This is Jimbo, Momma," she had said. And he stood at the foot of the bed smiling, wrapped his long arms around her daughter, said, "Don't you worry, Mrs. Jenkins, I'll take care of your little girl."

And with the way he smiled back then, anybody would believe him. He took good care of them both for a while, sneaking fried catfish dinners and hot fudge sundaes up to the hospital room. Sometimes she thought she would have given up if it hadn't been for Jimbo. There he was smiling, saying he'd take care of her girl. And he had kept them laughing with his stories of how he could walk into Penney's and walk out carrying a television, a rug, a bicycle if he wanted, right under the cashier's nose. Connie couldn't help laughing, couldn't help sitting back in her bed, couldn't help asking, "How do you do it, Jimbo?"

And he had grinned, said, "You just have to look like you know what you're doing. You just look like that little color TV belongs in your hand and you walk out that door, and that big-eyed little check-out girl just watches, while you say, 'Have a nice day ma'am.' And she says, 'Thank you.'" He had laughed, nudged Trisha's shoulder just a little too hard. Connie didn't like that laugh. He brought flowers and catfish and hot fudge sundaes, but she had heard that laugh before, knew the sound of danger, so she fought to keep on living to take care of her girl.

Connie finished the dishes and went back to the living room. Trisha lay flat on her back with the blanket pulled up and tangled around her neck. Connie carefully straightened the covers and pulled off Trisha's new shoes and took them to the closet so if Trisha wanted to leave, she would have to ask for her shoes. Connie picked up the leather jacket to hang, and thought of Trisha all dressed the way Jimbo dressed her like something out of a magazine: silk shirts, good leather, wool sweaters, and designer jeans. Whenever Connie complained about Jimbo, Trisha always said, "But Momma, look at all my pretty things." Now she heard Trisha snore, then mumble the slurred tangled words of a little girl dreaming. "Just sleep," Connie thought. She had always loved her baby most when she was sleeping.

Connie unplugged the phone and went to the kitchen. She decided to clean out what she called the junk drawer. Everything in the house that had no place to go found its way there: coupons, pencils, nails, string. She emptied the drawer on the table and sat with a fresh cup of coffee.

She wondered how so many odd things could wind up in the

drawer, as if they had sneaked in there of their own will: the imitation pearl earring she thought she had lost months ago, the piece of dried-up macaroni that must have slid off the counter, toothpicks, a perfume bottle, a hickory nut, the sample of fabric softener she got who knows when in the mail. She never remembered putting things in there, but somehow they piled up till one day she opened the drawer, looked in, thought, "How in the world have I been living around such a mess?"

She had always prided herself on keeping a good house. Even back when Larry kept her so scared she couldn't see straight, she had always found a way to keep the floor waxed and the windows clean. But a mess in a drawer always grew somehow, like a spider's web in a corner you couldn't reach. She leaned back from the table, closed her eyes, felt that old tangle of voices rise up in her head. She could hear him screaming, "Shut up, god damn you!" She could hear her own crying, "Stop, please, Larry!" She could see her little girl running in circles, shaking her hands like she was flinging something hot. She could hear that scream.

Connie sat up in the chair and tried to think of something else to clean. The house was still, quiet as a well, but all those voices kept screaming. She thought, "It's all right. It's all right. Your girl is sleeping, and the only real sound you hear is the refrigerator." She forced her mind to listen to that easy hum.

She heard Trisha moan. "Momma, Momma, I'm sick." Connie hurried to help Trisha to the bathroom. She sat by the toilet and soothed Trisha's head with a cold cloth while she vomited and cried.

Connie washed Trisha's face, helped her into a flannel nightgown, and led her back to the couch. "Water," Trisha said. Connie made a tall glass of ice water, placed it carefully between Trisha's hands, then sat in a chair and watched Trisha drink.

"You don't have to live like this," Connie said. She wanted to shake her, wanted to throw her against the wall and scream, "Why do you do this!"

"You think I'm happy?" Trisha said. "I know he'll do it again." She was crying. "He says he won't. He don't mean to hurt me, Momma. He loves me. He kisses me, Momma. When he kisses me sometimes, it's like sinking my mouth in a bowl of whipped cream." She covered her face with her hands. "You'll never know what I mean."

Connie reached for her, tried to rock her like a baby. Oh yes, she remembered those kisses before the black turn, kisses that spread across your mouth like cream. Connie gave her a tissue to wipe the lip that was bleeding again. "We aren't giving him another chance," she said. "You're leaving for good, this time. Remember?"

Trisha dabbed at her lip. "I guess I'll have to see him sometime." She looked at the floor. "He's got all my stuff. My clothes. My boots. My plants."

Connie stood to take the empty glass to the kitchen. "I'm coming with you this time," she said. "We'll walk in there together, get everything that's yours, right down to the knives and forks."

She held Trisha tightly, but Trisha shrugged her shoulders and pulled away. "He loves me, Momma. We have a real good time, sometimes. Like the other night he went out for pizza just because I was hungry. So we sat up in bed and ate pizza. See, Momma, he loves me." Trisha shook her head and stared at the floor. "He'd die for me, Momma. He said that once, he said, 'I'd die for you, girl. Would you die for me?' And he tickled me till I said yes. Oh Momma, you don't know how he can get me laughing. He tickled and tickled till I couldn't breathe, till I said, 'Yes, oh yes, Jimbo, I'd die for you.' And I would, Momma, 'cause I know he'd die for me."

"He's lying," Connie said.

Trisha sat back on the couch and pulled the blanket up around her. "It's your fault," she said. "If you weren't so sick, I wouldn't need Jimbo. I wouldn't need somebody to take care of me."

"I'm not sick!" Connie said.

"But you will be," Trisha said. "We all know it. You'll get sick again. And you'll die one day."

Connie reached for her, held her again, thinking she could hang on. She would hang on forever for Trisha. She owed her life to Trisha. It was Trisha who saved her that night when Larry had beaten her so badly she was passing out on the floor, and he started kicking, aiming for her head. Trisha had screamed and grabbed his leg, and he had tried to shake her off, but she held on until he grabbed her and threw her across the room.

That night Connie had taken Trisha and left, thinking, "You can hit me, Larry, but not my girl." She had hoped that by leaving the man she could leave it all like a bad dream, but he put his mark on Trisha. Trisha was still wearing the mark of a fist like a brand. A voice hissed in her head, "It's you, Larry. You're the reason my girl is sitting here on my couch bleeding." Connie stroked Trisha's hair. "I did all I could," she thought. "It was him that did this. I just loved a man who could hurt me." She took Trisha's hand and pulled it as if they were walking and Connie could pull her to the right way. "Don't love anybody that can hurt you, honey," she said, thinking, "The only safe love is a mother love." But she wouldn't say that because she knew better. Any kind of love was a danger.

She looked up and saw a face peering in the window, and she pulled Trisha close. She heard a rustle outside, then a step on the front porch.

Trisha sat up. "It's Jimbo," she whispered.

"Hush!" Connie said. She covered Trisha's shoulders with the blanket, then left the room to get the .38 out of her top drawer. She was ready. She would not let him win now. She wasn't sick and wouldn't die for a long time.

"Trisha!" Jimbo said. "I didn't mean to hurt you so bad, honey."

Trisha ran to the door, leaned against it and yelled, "You get away from me!"

Connie pulled Trisha from the door and turned on the porch light. "Leave her alone, Jimbo."

"This ain't your business," he said.

"I got my .38 pointed at the door," she said. "I can use it."

"No!" Trisha screamed.

"Don't fight her, Trisha," Jimbo said. "The gun might go off. She won't shoot."

Connie took a breath and stared at the gun in her hand, suddenly wondering if she really held a weapon. She thought, "How can he talk like that, so easy, like he was saying, 'Don't bump her arm, she might spill her coffee." Like being careful had nothing to do with staying alive. She yelled through the door. "You don't know me!" She waved her empty hand at Trisha, said, "Get over there and sit down."

"Now, Connie," Jimbo said. "You know I love Trisha. You know I don't want to hurt your girl."

She wouldn't listen to his words. She yelled, "Get away, Jimbo!" She thought, "Careful, don't let him get started on love." She forced her words over his deep, heavy voice. "Stay away from my girl!"

Trisha was pulling Connie's arm. "He just wants to talk." She leaned next to the window. "I'm listening, Jimbo. Just tell me you love me, Jimbo. Just say you love me, please."

Connie tried to pull Trisha's hand from the curtain, but Trisha wouldn't move. She and Jimbo stared at one another through the glass. Trisha's mouth was bleeding again, and Jimbo stood there, his handsome face calm, his dark eyes just a little bit worried, just sad enough to make you think he was sorry, just gentle enough to make you think he was safe. He was too good-looking, Connie thought, to get so mean.

She saw blood smeared on his green shirt with the alligator stitched on the front. He always wore those shirts and designer jeans. He liked to brag about those shirts he stole. She looked at his face, thought he looked like a sad little boy trying to look brave, the back straight, standing tall, but the mouth tight, the eyes looking down at some scary thing just there in the air between them. She forced her eyes to look at the blood on his shirt, not at the face of a sad boy. She stared hard at the dark stain of Trisha's blood on his shirt.

Trisha cried, "Go on, Jimbo. Tomorrow I'll come back and we can talk."

"I want you now!" he yelled. "I drove all the way out here!" He slapped his hand against the window. "God damn it, Trisha, you know I've been good to you."

Connie stepped back from the window, moved back toward the center of the living room to get away from the sight of that stain on his shirt, knowing if she looked long enough she would kill him. The gun was heavy in her hand, so heavy it pulled her arm, her shoulder, her whole body to a deep heavy place in the center of the room. Even if the house were burning down in that instant, she wouldn't be able to move. She saw Trisha reach, open the door, and heard the word "No!" jump from her mouth like a quick hard breath. The gun was so heavy. She tried to pull it up, hold it steady with both hands.

Jimbo stepped back from the open door. "Easy now, Connie. I'm not coming in." Trisha stood there holding the door knob, half leaning out toward Jimbo, but holding back to be safe from where his hand could reach. "Look at my face, Jimbo. Look what you did to me."

"I know what I did," he said in the quiet voice Connie hated. It made her shiver to hear a man talk as if he had the power to do anything, as if he were something more than a man that walked the earth on two legs and lived and died like everything else. But he did have a power with that voice. She had heard it in Larry, that deep man's voice that could make you put down the telephone when you were calling for help, that voice that wrapped around you like a rope, pulled you down, yanked at your chest while your feet carried you across the floor. Connie looked at Trisha, saw the voice work as her baby girl leaned against the door and cried.

Connie grabbed her under both arms and pulled her to the center of the living room. She felt strong, stronger than his voice as she turned and looked Jimbo in the face and said, "You leave her alone. I swear I'll blow your head off and tell the cops I thought you were a thief."

He looked down, shook his head. "I don't have to come in," he said. "Ask Trisha." He looked straight at Connie. "Ask Trisha if she wants to go."

Trisha was crying, crawling across the floor, looking for her shoes. Connie put the gun down in the corner of the room and gripped Trisha's arm and sat down beside her on the floor. She held her shoulders and tried to look into her daughter's eyes. She saw a swollen blotchy face that wasn't Trisha but some strange girl that stank with sweat and blood. "You don't have to go," Connie said. "In a few minutes he'll be gone, and I'll buy you all new stuff. I promise I'm gonna live a long time. I can do it, honey, I can live. Even the doctor said it's a matter of will."

Trisha shook her head and fought to get to the door. Connie looked up and saw Jimbo's face staring down at them. He looked peaceful. Even with the blood on his shirt, he looked happy as a man sitting on a bench and just watching the clouds change. He would wait all night if he had to because he knew he had the power. Connie cried, "Trisha, please!" She cringed at that old word, "Please," the sound that tore from her throat just before Larry had slammed her head against the wall. Trisha yanked her hands free, ran to the door, and was gone.

Connie sat on the floor and stared at the open door. Trisha had run off barefoot, with her nightgown flapping around her jeans. Connie saw the gun lying in the corner where she had put it down, out of the way, where it would do no harm. She had never even pushed back the safety catch.

She looked up at the door thrown open wide to the dark night. The house was still now. She couldn't remember when her head had felt so empty of human sound, those talking voices tangled and rushing, the old constant noise. She was empty now. Still. She heard tires screech somewhere in the distance. She heard crickets chirping loud and strong, the sound mixing with the pulse beating in her head, and she wondered if they had been singing like that while she and Trisha were screaming and Jimbo was talking so easy and winning just as he knew he would. The sound of the crickets filled the air, the house, her head, growing stronger, then fading, then stronger again, and she wondered how long had their song filled the night and how long would they sing. Connie strained to hear a human noise. Connie heard her heartbeat. She heard an owl scream in the trees.

Navigation

Lina had thought climbing the stone wall would be easy. She had slipped off her sandals and thrown them over first. Then, with her bare feet, she gripped the rough sandstone and jumped as she pulled her weight up with her arms. But her body hung there. It wouldn't move up, and she wouldn't let it slide down. She hung there. Michael was already on the other side, and she hated him there patiently waiting while she strained.

His ideas always sounded so simple: "Let's sneak in the park tonight. Let's spend the day in a cave. Let's sit on a mountain and watch the sun rise." It always sounded like an adventure, but whenever she got there, she fought an urge to run away or go to sleep. Now she hung against the wall. She groaned and pulled her body up, and with the weight of her chest on top of the wall, she pulled her legs up easily, balanced a moment, then dropped loosely, carefully to the darkness on the other side.

She brushed off her hands and looked up at him. He was pale in the moonlight, and the square lines of his face reminded her of the stone soldiers who stared determined while the rains and snows and winds beat their fierce and boyish faces. "I think I'm still in one piece," she said.

He returned her sandals. "Getting back over is the hard part," he said. "The wall is taller on this side."

Lina looked at the wall. He was right.

"The parking lot builds up the ground level on the other side." He patted her shoulder. "But don't worry. I can be helpful if you let me." She reached and held his arm as she slipped on her sandals. She let go and walked toward the center of the park on the north point of Lookout Mountain. Michael followed. He would let her lead.

They stood under tall oak trees and looked up. Lina saw flickers of starlight as she watched the leaves shift in the breeze. Beyond the park, where the mountain dropped to sandstone bluffs and wild flowering shrubs, she could see the city filling the valley with its glaring yellow and white streetlights. It all glimmered.

"Let's walk," Lina said as she headed for the narrow paved path along the edge of the mountain. She watched her feet as they moved. She knew she should ask him about his trip. It was Egypt, she thought. Maybe Morocco. Some exotic place full of dark-skinned people, where all the white people were rich, bright, light against the vast brown land. Michael said he loved those countries because he didn't belong. Lina thought only rich and safe people could want to go to a place where they didn't belong. He was always taking trips. His father's travel agency had free tickets.

She could hear him walking behind her. She didn't want to ask about his trip. He was always taking trips. "Go," she would say. "Just go. Give me some time." So he went, and he returned, and she always wanted him back.

She wanted him, his voice, his mouth, the feel of his hands, but after a time, she always said, "Go." She pulled back and said, "Go." And he would go and return, and wait for her sign.

She listened to the sound of his running shoes on the pavement. She could see the way he ran across a track, long stride, back straight, chin steady and up. He was lean and strong. He was patient, good to her. He loved her. He would always return. She turned to look at him in the dim light and wondered why.

She stopped at the edge of the path and looked out. Lights of the bridge across town arched against the sky as if they lighted the path of a roller coaster beginning in bright light, trailing into darkness.

Michael stood beside her. "I'm tired of traveling," he said. "I go and come back. You go and come back."

She shrugged. "I don't go anywhere."

"You go into yourself. You're always leaving me, even when I've got you in my hands." He held her wrist.

She let him hold her, then she stepped over the small chain fence that served as a reminder that visitors should stay on the path. She walked away. She knew she loved this man. She had held him, and he had moved in her like a wave. But sometimes when he touched her, she felt as if her body were made of clay. Soft. Cold. Dead. She moved away. She found the broad flat rock she usually claimed on sunny afternoons. She had always liked to sit there between the valley and the hard mountain. She liked to watch the tourists grinning and sighing from other rocks along the bluffs. The sandstone outcroppings were secure, but they offered danger, so people from as far away as New York or Japan could have some of the mountain's wildness, could feel daring, sense danger. They could gasp at the light, the broad vision of earth, rock, trees, birds, sky, and yet they could feel secure and safe in front of someone's camera.

But now, there were no tourists, just Michael who had a way of leading her to places where she had to think. Any other man would have led her there to pull at her clothes, but she knew a body was an easy thing to give, just a few buttons and the skin sighs out. Michael didn't just want her body. He wanted her to fill all his empty places, and she didn't have enough. She was broken glass scattered in bright sharp lights across a floor. She couldn't fill anyone's spaces. "You can see Polaris clearly from here," Michael said. "The guide star. I always wanted to fly to stars."

Lina looked at the steady hard light of Polaris. She looked down at the city lights and thought they were somehow more distant, more alien than any star. "Stick to the earth a little longer," she said. "Stars burn." He looked at her. She knew he would touch her, and he did. His hand was cool and dry, soft as a woman's yet strong, as if his hands were meant for holding delicate tools. She leaned toward him and held her breath. She smelled his skin like leaves, like night, and she stepped away.

"God, I love this place." He was standing with his arms crossed as he looked out at the city. "There are a lot of stories about this mountain," he said. "No one knows all the stories. It's full of ghosts, you know. Lives lived, layers and layers of life buried here. Like fossils."

Lina nodded. She knew the stories. "I like the one about the Lula Lake woman. She walks the bluffs overlooking the water and cries for her drowned baby."

"Too romantic," Michael said. "It's got no originality. How many crying ghost lady stories have you heard? Dozens. It's a cliché."

Lina thought of all the stories, the ghostly women waiting on mountains, under bridges, walking down railroad tracks, crying from woods, attics, cellars, caves. She thought that if all those stories were true, the land would scream with the sound of wailing women.

"I know better stories." Michael said.

"Tell me." She loved his stories, loved to lie back and let his voice roll over her, loved to feel the sound of him move inside her own skin. She sat, pulled her knees up to her chest, and looked out at the dark river at the base of the mountain. The winding stretch of water was called Moccasin Bend because of the way the river bent around a small peninsula on the opposite shore. It formed a shape similar to an Indian moccasin. She was sure there was a story to the name, and she was sure he knew it. But when she looked down, she didn't want to hear stories made to explain the shape of land and water. On that peninsula she saw the mental hospital. She had been there. She had seen the stories behind the fences, the bright lights, green walls. Surrounded by dark water and thick woods, the hospital lights shone with a constant dull glare. Any tourist might admire the view of the well-trimmed, neatly designed grounds on the edge of the river, anyone who didn't know there were men and women trapped down there behind the light. Inside those walls were stories, stories he would never comprehend.

He knew she had been there, but he didn't know why. He

didn't know Lina, the woman who crashed like glass, splintered into points, all light reflecting, no center, no form, the crazed Lina who crawled on all fours and screamed up at the white ceiling pressing down smashing, shattering her glass skin, Lina staring up, screaming, on the floor and screaming, "Let me out! Let me out!"

She stared down at the dull light across the river. She knew she was healed. The crash was years ago, and they had found her pieces, almost all of her, and she remade her form. She was whole now. She walked, talked, breathed, like any person. She was whole now, but she could slip. Michael was a wind, a wave she wanted to ride, but she could slip. Careful. She would not slip. That was years ago, and she was healed. He knew she had come through what they called a rough time, a bad time, as if a past time would stay past. But that time was with her always. Michael thought madness was a thing you forgot, but Lina knew it stayed. She carried it like a scar.

He sat beside her. "I can tell you war stories."

"Tell me a story about people. I don't want history. Tell me about people who want something they can't have."

"I can tell you about the men who died for this mountain. Hopeful young men scattered on the ground."

She shook her head. "Ideals. Honor. Sacrifice. I want a human story."

"The men bleed. They cry. It's a human story."

"I'll listen." The story didn't matter. She wanted to hear his voice.

He waved his hands over the grass. "There was a battle here. They called it The Battle Above the Clouds."

Lina smiled. "Of course. High on Mount Olympus in Chattanooga, Tennessee. Boy-gods fighting above the clouds."

"No. Listen." He touched the back of her hand. "It was a gray day. Full of mist. They say when the Union soldiers moved up the side of the mountain, clouds gathered and parted as quickly as the troops. Where the clouds parted you could see the men rushing forward, a path of blue motion rushing forward, up in the mist. Sometimes they had to scramble up precipices, straining with hands and feet. They tore down barricades and pushed ahead in blue waves through the gray white clouds. They climbed faster with each yard."

She jabbed him. "You make it sound like a football game."

He looked at her. "The camps were strewn with dead and mangled bodies. Is that what you want?"

"No. Just don't give me glory. You see passion, action, romance. I see dead men. Blood and flies, not clouds moving up a mountain."

"You have no sense of history."

"I don't need it." She stood and walked away, knowing he would be just behind her. She walked quickly to a clearing where two cannons sat poised as if ready to fire into the valley. She had seen children here, squealing, leaping, wild as goats. They always had their pictures taken while they grinned, straddling a cannon as if it were a rocket they could ride to the moon. She rested her back against the cold metal and looked out at the blinking lights.

He followed her. He leaned against the other cannon and waited. She spoke softly. "Sometimes I wonder why we even talk about love. Why bother? We don't have much in common. You and your trips, your money, your place in the world. You fit. Me? My whole family's crazy or dead. I'm from another planet."

"You're not cursed." He reached for her.

"You're not listening."

"You're not trying."

"I don't want to try." She wanted him to hold her. She wanted to walk away.

He stepped back and crossed his arms. "We can't leave each other alone. You know that."

"I know." She reached for him. She held him. She pressed her head to his chest and felt the soft cotton cloth of his shirt, his warmth. She listened. "Don't move," she said. She held him and closed her eyes. "Talk to me," she said. "Let me hear your voice. Talk to me."

He rubbed her back with his wide open hands. "I'll tell you another story. You'll like this one. It's got real people. A man and his wife, his friends. All going down a river. It's got suspense. Maybe even devils. You like those ghost and devil stories."

"I like people stories," she said.

"People stories always have ghosts and devils of some kind."

She smiled and stepped away. "Let's walk down to the point and watch the river. You can tell me the story then take me home. All right?" He nodded. She nudged him forward. "You lead the way."

Michael knew the mountain. He had played there all his life. He knew each tree, where the sidewalk ended, where damp moss or loose rocks could cause a slip. They walked down the sloping path, the steps, then the winding walkway through the woods.

They came to a small bricked promontory. When the park was open to tourists, a recorded voice loudly explained the battles that took place below the mountain, and a massive screen illuminated with colored lights depicted troop movements across the valley. The complexities of war were made clear in red and blue dots of light that led a precise pathway over the cool aluminum and glass map of the South. In the dark the screen stood over them, a silent shape that did nothing but absorb moonlight.

He led her off the walkway to an outcropping of sandstone where they had a clear view of the river. The yellow-white hospital lights glowed at the bend. Farther down the river, the harsher lights of the steel foundry, the slaughterhouse, and the paper mill glared through clouds of smoke and steam.

Lina sat and watched the lights flicker and fade. Michael sat beside her, but not too close. He wouldn't touch her. He always knew when to leave her alone.

"Down there in the river is a whirlpool." He spoke as if he were sitting in a circle of listeners, as if his words held secrets that would be known only when his voice had stopped. "The early navigators called that place the Boiling Pot. They said it took in trees, boats, anything, and spewed them out again half a mile away."

Lina smiled. "I think I'm going to like this."

He nodded. "Naturally a pilot came along who swore he could get his boat down that river 'smooth as goose grease.' He said he would take his wife for good luck, and he would take his best men, and they would beat that river. They would have a few drinks, toast the moon, which was full, of course. They would have a pleasant ride. So they put in up river on a sunny afternoon, and he set to work. He was a very proud and competent man."

"Of course," Lina said.

"All was going fine. And then night came. They kept sliding down the river. They had supper. A few shots of whiskey. All was going smooth."

"As goose grease?" she said.

He smiled. "They were moving along, real peaceful. Then far away on shore they saw a house with the lights up and music playing across the water. They raised their drinks to the party and kept gliding in the dark. Then they passed another house with the lights up and the same happy tune playing.

"The pilot and his crew toasted the party and moved on. They passed another house with lights up, same tune playing, and they declared the riverside the jolliest, dancingest place in the country.

"Then, more darkness. Another house came up with the party growing louder and that same tune playing fast. Then darkness. They saw that house again and again and again. The pilot started getting nervous. He decided either the whole crew was drunk or some hellish thing was following them down the river."

Lina smiled. Michael was silent. He knew how to hold her. When to hold, when to let go.

"When the pilot saw the next house coming up, he called his wife on deck because she was the only one sober. And she saw the same house, heard the same noise. She held his hand and said, 'Yes, something is there.' The pilot got real nervous. He said the next time they passed this house, they would go in and tie up the boat to see what was real. So when they saw it again, they docked and walked toward the light. And they saw the party was nothing but real men, real women, and even real children dancing along. No magic. No spirits. They were all eating real food and playing songs everyone on the boat knew the words to. No tricks, no devils, just a bunch of people having a good time in the dark.

"The pilot figured that they had been stuck on the current of the Boiling Pot. They had been going around and around, watching the same dark, with the same lights passing by. The pilot laughed, they all laughed, and they had another whiskey and swore that the night was like a dream."

Lina leaned and kissed him just at the temple where his hair was soft, and she could feel his skin. 'That's a real story," she said. She took his hand and held it to her mouth, touched it with her lips. He smelled like leaves, like a river, like stone. She breathed.

They watched the river curve below as they listened to the wind in the trees. The red, blue, orange, and yellow-white lights of the city glowed in a vague and distant cloud. She saw a jet come in and descend over the ridge across the valley. She watched it circle to land with its lights flickering to signal anyone below that it was coming in. She knew that on the other side of the ridge in a field of blue light, people on the ground were flashing lights back to the pilot, sending messages through the air. He would land smoothly and safely. She sighed as the jet disappeared.

"I guess you want to go now," he said.

"No. Not yet."

"How many trips will I have to make before you really want me back. I keep saying that I'll go off and stay, and I believe it when I say it. But I keep coming and going like a god-damned tide, going out, coming in. Just like the water, something pushes me back in."

"I need more time," she said.

He stood. "I'm not proposing marriage. I just want you to be here when I hold you."

She closed her eyes. She wanted to be there too.

"Is it so hard?"

She nodded.

"Let's go." He walked away, but she wouldn't move. She couldn't move. She knew if she followed him now and got back in the car, she would be locked in, trapped behind glass, like a white moth beating filmy wings against a jar. "Let me out," she thought. She shook her head. No. She was out. She could smell the trees. She stood and called to him. She saw him stop, and turn, his shirt bright in the shadows, his face, there. "Not yet," she said. Did he hear her voice? He was coming, and she moved toward him now. She would hold his arm, feel his skin, the blood pulse over muscle, bone.

She wrapped her arms around him. "You feel good," she whispered. "Don't go yet."

"I'm not going anywhere," he said. He rubbed the back of her neck.

She took his hand and walked back to the point. "Come talk to me. I want to hear you. Tell me that story again. I want to close my eyes and see the water swirl. Say it again. Say anything. I want to hear your voice."

They sat. He looked out at the city while she lay down and looked up through the trees. She watched his face in the light. She pulled him to her, kissed him. She pulled him closer, kissed hard, deep. She could feel him, smell him. She listened to his heart as he lay beside her and held her. He closed his eyes, and breathed.

She slid her hand in his shirt and pressed, felt his skin with her stretched fingers, the palm of her hand. His hands moved and his mouth pressed. He smelled like water. She pulled him to her. She could feel him. She was there. Hands, mouth, skin sighing, yes, body bending like a leaf toward light.

She closed her eyes. She could see the woman on the river, where she held her husband, the pilot, and they looked out from the boat rocking on the river. The night was black, and the silver river moved fast. They stood and watched the trees, the hills, the land rushing by. She heard music on the water, pulsing high happy music rising off the water. She held him, said "What's that noise. I hear a tune rippling in the dark." And they looked, listened. She saw the light in the darkness. There. She wanted to mark the place so she would know where she had been, but the light slipped away.

She knew she was in a dangerous place where the land changed its shape, where whirlpools turned all around, where the water pulled you under, carried you down. She knew there was a risk, and she wanted to be certain of her way. She could feel him. She could hear his voice whispering her name. She was there. She could smell the land, feel the water, warm swirling rising water, pulling her down as he moved in her, and her body broke and rushed toward the light.

The Evil Side
of Red Brown

The smell of his smoke is killing me. It made Momma sick, and it makes me sick too. It clogs up your eyes and throat, and he sits there puffing.

I know I could ask him to open his window, but I won't because then he'd know I have a weak spot, a weak spot worth talking about. So I open my window a crack, and I lean and try to breathe a little fresh air. But the window being open on my side just makes it worse. I can't win. And he sits over there driving this old pickup like he's king of the road, and he puffs that cigar just making me sick.

"Not much traffic," he says, staring out at the empty highway.

"Yeah," I say. "It's like that when you leave early in the morning." Last night he said if we leave early, there won't be much traffic, and this morning, while we sat drinking coffee and looking out at the dark, he said there won't be much traffic, and now he says it again. Am I supposed to act like it's some big surprise or what?

Why couldn't they let me fly home in peace? I was in a plane once, and I loved it. Flying, being in the middle of all those people going places, and the nice talk about nothing, eating those peanuts in little packages and drinking Seven-Up. That's nice. And you look down and see nothing but clouds and clouds. People on the plane talk real quiet. They nod and smile and eat their snacks. I like that.

"You need anything?" he says.

"No, I'm fine," I say.

At least on this trip he's thinking about something besides himself. I can remember going on trips with him where me and Carly would have to sit in the back seat with our legs crossed so tight it hurt. We'd sit like that real quiet, just waiting on him to stop. And he wouldn't stop for nothing. Momma would say, "Red, please." And he'd say, "We haven't been going that long. They can wait." And me and Carly would look at Momma and wait, and Daddy would drive on, smoking that cigar just like he is now. So I do like I did then: keep my face close to the window and watch the land go by.

Even if it is early, even if his smoke is killing me, and even if it is so quiet in this truck I could scream, I can't help but notice that the morning sun on these Pennsylvania mountains is something special. If anybody else were sitting in that driver's seat, I'd say so. But you don't talk about mountains and sunlight to Daddy. I doubt he even notices. But Momma would notice. She loves mountains, says gods live in mountains. I've told her that at church they say only Indians believe gods live in mountains, and their souls are damned. But she says no, Christians can believe in mountain gods too.

Daddy gets mad when she talks like that. He beats her for it sometimes. Especially if he's been drinking. When Daddy's been drinking, he does one or two or all of three things: beats on the nearest living thing, cries and pees on himself, or tells jokes about black people. I guess he's always mad, or feeling sorry for himself, or trying to feel like he's got one up on something.

One day in her Sunday school class they were talking about, I guess I should say against, black people in white churches, and Momma opened her mouth and said, "How do we know if God ain't black or green or polka-dot?" The town of Copper Hill never forgave her for that one. Of course they forgot about the green and polka-dot part and called her a nigger lover. She was only teaching us what was right. When I die and find out that God is polka-dot and lives in a mountain, I won't be too surprised.

"You ought to keep your eyes peeled for some deer," he says. I look at him. "Lots of them get hit by cars this time of year." I look out at the road and look back at him. "It'll sure mess up your car to hit one of those things," he says.

"What about the deer?" I say.

He smiles around his cigar and nods. "Mess up that deer too."

How can you enjoy a ride with a man who talks like that? Even if he is your daddy. Especially if he's your daddy. At least, thank the Lord, on this trip he isn't drinking. He promised Momma, and me twice, he wouldn't. And one thing about him, he keeps his promises. He just doesn't make many.

Sitting here, looking at him—wrinkled, gray, too fat, too tired to fight—I wonder how much he remembers. And I want to remind him of the side of him no one wants to talk about. The evil side. Like the time he took a shot at Momma and buckshot splattered all over the dining-room wall. To this day those holes are still in that wall, and no one talks about them. Or the time he threw the cat so hard its head squashed. They couldn't stop me from screaming, and Momma stood there with her hand over her mouth saying, "Oh, Red. Oh, Red." Or the morning we found Momma's brand new dishwasher out in the yard with its door twisted off. Momma cried over that one. But Momma says since she's been sick, he's a new man. If you ask me, it's a crying shame that it takes her getting sick and dying to make him change. Maybe he's realizing that the battle with Momma is about over and there's no way anybody can really win. So maybe he's just trying to enjoy the little bit that is left. Nah, he's probably just worrying about his own dying. Can't fool me.

Suddenly the truck slows and Daddy leans forward. "There's one," he says. I see it laying on the side of the road. It looks like it could be a doe. Her front legs stick in the air like she was frozen in a run. We ride by, staring, then Daddy shifts his cap, raises his eyebrows and says, "That's a waste of good meat back here."

I want to yell, "That's a waste of good life back there," but I nod and say, "Yeah." And I'm thinking all that deer was trying to do was get to a new place, a pretty place, a safe place with clear water, food, maybe a fresh salt lick. Just trying to get by is all. Then wham! Some car just trying to get by too ends it all right there. Nobody sees it coming, then wham!

He's sitting up straighter now. His old red cap is pushed back on his head, and he leans over the steering wheel and looks out. I can see his eyes shine. He has that same look when he watches a pretty blond waitress, and he probably had the same look in his eyes the first time he saw Momma. And I'm sure he looks that way when he's in the woods thinking of all the wild things. He says, "I'd love to be in those mountains right now."

I knew it. Let him see something bleeding, and he's ready to hunt. "You just love to shoot things," I say as mean as I dare.

He leans back, and his hands loosen a little on the steering wheel. "Yeah," he says. "Lets you know you're alive to go for a deer. You've got to be sneaky, fast, and tough to get one." The last thing I want to hear is what a man you have to be to shoot a deer. Next thing I know, he'll be telling me what a man you have to be to shoot at your wife.

Momma used to go deer hunting too. Momma and Daddy and a couple of Daddy's friends used to go together, always after the first frost, when the snakes go in. They'd leave me and Darly at Grandma's house. And we'd pray that somehow the wild things would stay alive and free. But a lot of good praying does. When Daddy brought home that ten-point buck, me and Carly cried and cried. Of course Momma was proud of that buck. A good wife is supposed to be, I guess. But Momma didn't hunt. Momma went deer hunting because she liked the mountains. She liked the woods and the streams and the trees all shimmering with fall colors. She would bring me back bright leaves, dried weeds, and shiny rocks called fool's gold. I still have a box of fool's gold I saved from Momma's trips to the mountains.

Momma taught me to always look at the good things in life. "Life's a matter of what you're looking at," she always said. Daddy saw deer to shoot at; Momma saw mountains. What she saw in Daddy, I'll never know. She couldn't understand why I left home so young. I saw something in Daddy she didn't, I guess. So as soon as I could raise the money for a one-way ticket I headed north to the Pennsylvania mountains and my crazy Aunt Spokey. Daddy said I must be as nuts as she is.

We started out calling her Aunt Spookey because she says she talks with the dead. But we changed it to Spokey because it sounds more polite. I guess I'm happy living with Aunt Spokey. At least it's peaceful. The only people that come around are the dead ones, and I've never been bothered by them. I've never seen one, even though she swears they come in and move her stamps and hide her hairbrush. She's strange all right. But we have our ways of having fun. We've got goldfish, guppies, and four parakeets that are free to fly around as they please. Parakeets and fish don't do much harm to nothing in this world. That's why we like them.

Daddy leans forward again, and the truck slows. I think that we're going to stare at another dead deer, then I see the green Buick setting crooked with a flat tire on the side of the road. I figure he's checking to see if a good-looking blonde is driving, so maybe he can play like the Lone Ranger and save the poor thing. If she is ugly, he is sure to pass her by. Daddy slows for a good peek, and we see a bent little old man clinging to his car like it was some kind of life raft.

Daddy doesn't say a word. He just pulls over and stops. I can't figure it out because there isn't even a woman in the car. "I'll be back in a minute," he says. Then he's gone. In the rear-view mirror, I watch him throw down that cigar, shove his hands in his pockets, and nod at the old man. I figure Daddy is saying he'll change the tire for a few dollars, but from what I can see, they're acting real friendly. Daddy is standing there nodding and even smiling, and the old man is leaning against his car, shrugging and waving one hand around, trying to explain what happened to his tire, I guess.

Next thing I know, Daddy is in the old man's trunk and pulling out a jack. So I pull out a stick of Juicy Fruit and start chewing. When I look up again, Daddy is talking to the old man and pointing to the truck. Lord, I hope that old man doesn't want to come sit in the truck with me. I know he's old and probably needs to sit, but I don't know what to say to an old man. It would be just like Daddy to tell him to come sit in here, with no thought at all of whether I'd like it.

Thank goodness the old man is shaking his head. He's probably thinking it wouldn't look right for him to be sitting in a truck with a girl while Daddy is out there doing the man's work. Men. I swear.

When I look up again, the old man is trying to give Daddy some money, and Daddy is standing there shaking his head. I can almost hear him saying "Nahh." He says "Nahh" to just about everything. You want some breakfast, Daddy? He says "Nahh." You work hard today, Daddy? "Nahh," he says. Like nothing don't mean nothing, he's got an answer for everything: "Nahh."

So the old man gets back into his car, and Daddy is hopping back into the truck before I know it. I watch him pull a rag out from under the seat, and I can see where he's hit his knuckle pretty hard on something, and it's bleeding. "Can I get you anything for that?" I say. "I've got some band-aids in my pocketbook."

"Nahh," he says, and he keeps wiping his hands. Of course. He wouldn't feel like a man if he let me do something. He lights up a fresh cigar and watches the old man pull out on the road. "Somebody's got to take care of the old ones," he says. And it rings in my head like something familiar, and I think for a minute I've seen him do this before. But it must have been a dream. Daddy eases his truck into gear, and we're rolling again.

I've asked Aunt Spokey why she wasn't scared of those dead people she talks to. She just smiles her wicked smile and says, "It's the living ones you've got to watch out for." Aunt Spokey doesn't trust people much, and she positively hates men. She says they're the cause of all evil. Of course I know the real reason she hates men. It's because the man she was supposed to marry went off to war and married some Japanese girl. Sometimes I still hear her muttering, "He wants to sit on the floor and eat raw fish, he can have it!" I guess she is a little crazy, but I feel sorry for her. And it sure beats living with Daddy.

So Aunt Spokey never married. Instead she started studying on ghosts, and spirits, and other-worldly things. She says Momma is a fool for staying with Daddy. She doesn't know how her own sister can be so blind to a way out of pain. Momma says it's love, but I think Momma has love and pain a little mixed up. I've told her, but she just cries.

I hope I can lead Carly to my way of thinking, before she signs her life away to pain. She says I'm too hard on Daddy, that I ought to come home and love him like a daughter should. I guess she doesn't see the Red Brown I do.

She was too young to see the worst. I did my best to hide it. I'd send her to the neighbor's house until we got Daddy to pass out. Or I'd set her up in the bedroom with the TV blaring loud. But sometimes she heard things. I ran away, but she stayed and learned to take it somehow.

It's got to mess up a girl, I think, to make her get used to a woman crying and a man blacking eyes, breaking arms, and busting holes in walls like that's the way it's supposed to be. I might not be the smartest person, but I know it doesn't have to be like that. She thinks Daddy is fine, that he's just a little mixed up. Lord! Even if Momma says he's changing, his fixing one flat tire doesn't change years of remembering. To change memories, you have to change facts, and the facts are fixed in my mind.

"There's another one," he says real loud. I don't know how much more of this I can take—his wishing he'd been the one to kill that deer instead of it being an accident. The way he stares at the thing makes me shiver. It makes him feel good to go driving by a dead thing while he can just go along healthy and strong. "That's a nice one," he says. He shakes his head, and he flicks his ashes on the floor.

"You love it, don't you," I yell.

He looks at me like he doesn't know what I'm talking about.

"You love shooting things. Killing."

He shrugs, shifts his cap on his head and says, "Honey, the world would be overrun with deer if somebody didn't hunt. It keeps 'em balanced."

I can't stand looking in the rear-view mirror at that deer sprawled dead on the highway. I say, "And I guess the world would be overrun with women if men didn't take shots at them now and then too."

Daddy slows the truck, it seems with the sole purpose to turn and frown at me. Then he tries to look like he doesn't know what I mean. "So you're just doing your job," I say. "I guess you took a shot at my momma just to keep a balance." I watch him press his lips together and shake his head. "Are you crazy or what?" I say.

He looks at me. "So one day I just picked up a gun and shot at your momma. No reason. For the hell of it, huh?" He looks back at the road and drives.

"Why?" I say.

He says real quiet and slow, "You think I did that. For no reason."

"I remember the holes," I say. "The holes in the dining room wall." He nods. "Weren't you ever sorry?" I say.

"We were both sorry," he says. He frowns and shifts in his seat. "We were both sorry," he says again.

"She's got nothing to be sorry for but putting up with you, for staying with a man who beat her, who tried to shoot her."

"You remember those holes, all right," he says, all of a sudden loud. "But you don't want to talk about why, do you?"

I stare out the window and wonder how I could get started on this with at least five hundred miles to go. And all for a deer. But I say real mean, "You've got a good reason, I guess."

He squashes his cigar in the ashtray and says, "I did what any man would do who caught his wife screwing that long-haired bastard from the corner store."

I think the word "screwing," and I feel the sickening hate of the sound. And I feel the shiver you feel when you're sitting peaceful in the morning sun, drinking a cup of coffee, and a nightmare out of nowhere creeps in your head. And I remember. I remember that time like so many other times. And I feel sick and frozen and falling like this must be a dream. And I see the bedroom door crash open and I hear the noise.

"I blew up!" Daddy yells.

He must be wrong. He must have it all wrong. But I'm seeing Charlie hanging around the kitchen, blue-eyed Charlie who worked nights at the corner store, handsome Charlie with the boots and the long hair, Charlie eating a big piece of rhubarb pie, and Momma standing there in her apron laughing. Having fun.

And I see Charlie sitting on the porch playing his harmonica, and me and Carly and Momma too, tapping our toes and singing. Just having fun was all, I want to yell. But I can see the bedroom door.

"I guess you chose to forget about that," Daddy says. And I'm trying to think it was all in good fun, and "forget about that" is ringing in my head.

Daddy is driving faster, and I want to yell, "Hold on! Slow down!" And the mountains and the trees go whizzing by. I look at Daddy and I see him like I saw him then, grabbing Momma by the hair and slinging her across the room and her screaming.

And blam! Momma falling to the floor like she was dead, and Charlie running out the back door. "Daddy stop!" I remember screaming. "Daddy stop!" And I hear that I'm talking out loud. Daddy slows down the truck and eases to the side of the road.

He sits there looking at me, and I think he's going to cry. "We were both sorry. Sorry as hell, and it's you girls that pay for it."

"Daddy." I say. I look into his face, wrinkled, broken down, tired.

"It'll be different now," he says.

"Oh, Daddy," I say. "It's too late. You're too old and she's too sick." He shakes his head and takes out a fresh cigar. I can already smell it, and I wonder how Momma took it all those years. "Who knows about what happened?" I say. "Did anybody know?"

"Not a damned soul," he says.

I look at him and I wonder how he could hold it in so tight and so long. And like he can hear what I'm thinking, he says, "I buried it. I beat hell out of her, and I buried it." He starts up the truck and looks at me. "You all right? You gonna be sick or something?"

"No," I say. "My stomach's kind of turning, but let's go."

He pulls onto the road. "Up ahead we'll get you some ice cream." Of course. He thinks ice cream and whiskey will cure everything. I think I ought to ask him if he's all right, if he needs something, but he'd probably want a drink. I watch him suck that cigar that I hate, and I remember I hate, and I want to say, "If you hadn't beat her all those years—" but I know he must be wondering about all those years too, and what they mean since she's dying now.

So I look out the window and watch the colors on the mountains. I wish those mountain gods would speak and tell me who to blame for a family like mine. But the mountains just stand there, strong and green by the highway. I watch, and I think of my fish swimming golden and quiet and my bright parakeets flying through the house, and I say nothing.